The Book of Want

Camino del Sol
A Latina and Latino Literary Series

The Book of Want

Daniel A. Olivas

THE UNIVERSITY OF ARIZONA PRESS
TUCSON

The University of Arizona Press
© 2011 Daniel A. Olivas
All rights reserved

www.uapress.arizona.edu

Library of Congress Cataloging-in-Publication Data
Olivas, Daniel A.
  The book of want : a novel / Daniel A. Olivas.
    p. cm. — (Camino del sol)
  ISBN 978-0-8165-2899-8 (pbk. : alk. paper)
  1. Mexican Americans—Fiction. I. Title.
  PS3615.L58B66 2011
  813'.6–dc22
                                        2010026457

Publication of this book is made possible in part by the proceeds of a permanent
endowment created with the assistance of a Challenge Grant from the National
Endowment for the Humanities, a federal agency.

Manufactured in the United States of America on acid-free, archival-quality
paper containing a minimum of 30% postconsumer waste and processed
chlorine free.

16   15   14   13   12   11   6   5   4   3   2   1

For Sue and Ben

But a man never knows what he wants, what's good for him, what he should do. Fate hurries him like a witch into mistakes and heartaches. Nobody does what's good for them.

—Daniel Fuchs, *Low Company*

Love is an attempt at penetrating another being, but it can only succeed if the surrender is mutual.

—Octavio Paz, *The Labyrinth of Solitude*

Contents

Prologue: The Law Giver   xiii

1. Other Gods   1
2. Has He Been There for You?   13
3. Domingo   21
4. How to Date a Flying Mexican   29
5. The Dreamer   39
6. Los Dos   47
7. El Cucuy   57
8. Belén   65
9. Yahrzeit   79
10. Want: A Symphony   93

Epilogue   119

Acknowledgments

Portions of this novel previously appeared, sometimes in different form, in the following literary journals and are reprinted here by permission of the author: *OnePageStories* (2007); *Exquisite Corpse* (2008); *New Madrid* (2008); *Pembroke Magazine* (2008); *Tertulia Magazine* (2008); the *Los Angeles Times* (2010); *The Homeboy Review* (2010).

Though I know that it is impossible to thank all who have helped make this novel a reality, let me try:

Mil gracias to the wonderful people at the University of Arizona Press who not only agreed to publish my manuscript, but who also put great care into its editing, design, and promotion. Your dedication to Latino and Chicano literature is appreciated beyond words.

A nod to the many wonderful and dedicated authors I've had the honor to know throughout the years who have encouraged and supported my literary endeavors. In particular, I acknowledge my fellow blogueros y blogueras on *La Bloga* who never fail to cheer me on.

A shout-out to my friends at the California Department of Justice who have read my books and attended my various book readings. You have helped me integrate my life as a lawyer with my life as an author.

I thank my parents, who always made certain that the house was filled with books even when money was tight. You taught your children the joy of reading and the magic in books.

And finally, I must thank my wife, Susan Formaker, and our son, Ben: You two are my joy, my light, and my inspiration. I hope that you enjoy this novel, which I dedicate to you.

Prologue

The Law Giver

Conchita kicked her legs back and forth as they dangled from the edge of the chair. She fingered pieces of tamales de puerco past her greasy lips and happily hummed a nondescript melody. Belén stood by the woodstove and prepared a fresh cigarette. She liked them fat, bulging with tobacco. She watched her daughter eat and wondered how a four-year-old girl could consume as much as Conchita did without becoming a gordita. Belén licked one end of the now-full paper and rolled it until it resembled a boa constrictor that had just consumed a large dog or baby goat. She placed the cigarette between her lips, bent toward the oven, and puffed noisily as she lit it from a tiny flame that danced through one of the four round holes on the stovetop. Belén pulled back and stood as straight as she could. She scratched her bloated belly and wondered if this baby would be born alive, unlike the last three. A few more weeks and she'd know. As Belén took a long drag on her cigarette, she watched Conchita lift the plate to her mouth and lick up the remaining onion-and-cilantro sauce.

"¡Ay!" said Belén through a cloud of white smoke. "We're not poor, mija. You don't have to eat like you haven't had a bite in days!"

Conchita put the plate down and smiled. She then reached for her cup of hot coffee and carefully took a drink. Even at this young age, Belén could see that her daughter would grow to be a beautiful woman who enjoyed life. Belén wondered if her next one would be a boy. The three that God took before they could take a breath were all girls. The odds were in favor of a son. And that's what Celso wanted. Her husband adored Conchita but he desperately wanted a boy to take his name and follow him into the good-paying work at the Velasco ranch, which had some of the best cattle in the state of Jalisco. Hard work, to be sure, but Celso had been able to feed and clothe his growing family with some money left over for those extras that made life more than comfortable. They never wanted for anything even though the Great Depression and World War II had taken their toll on so many others. Life was good.

The morning sun came through the large window hard and bright. It was only seven in the morning but Celso had already been out the door and working for more than two hours. As Belén puffed away, she kept her eyes on Conchita. Her daughter's welfare weighed her down all morning because of that dream. Belén's late mother, Mónica, had spoken to her last night. Belén turned her mother's words round and round in her mind trying to decipher the message. For some reason, the dead spoke in riddles. Belén vowed that when she left this world and visited her loved ones in dreams, she would speak clearly and never ever obfuscate. What's the use of warning a daughter by communicating in code? Is this how the dead entertained themselves or tested the intelligence of their listeners? Or did God set up strict rules by which the dead were allowed to visit? Who knows. But all Belén understood at that moment was that her mother had given a warning of some type that concerned Conchita.

In the dream, Mónica had told Belén, "Your hija must listen to Moses, the law giver." She also added another odd tidbit: "Remember my name by putting me in the middle."

Nonsense.

No. The dead visit for a reason.

The baby kicked. And then it came to Belén as if she'd read it in a newspaper, if she could read. She rubbed her belly and grinned. This baby would be a girl, she realized. And they would name her Mónica. So simple! How could she not have seen it sooner? Celso would be disappointed but they could always try for a son next time. A healthy baby, even a girl, was a gift from God. Period.

Now for the other mystery. Conchita must listen to Moses? Belén puffed on her cigarette. Moses? Moses. Oh. Yes. Yes! That's it! She walked to the table and sat down next to Conchita.

"Mija," began Belén. "I want to tell you a story."

Conchita put the cup down, faced her mother, and offered wide-eyed attention.

"Mija," Belén said, now that her daughter listened intently, "I want to tell you a story about a great man who went up a mountain to talk to God."

"Was he a nice man?"

"Yes," said Belén. "He was old and nice and he loved his people."

"He sounds like Papá, except Papá isn't so old."

"Yes," she said, as she patted Conchita's arm. "Now let me tell you more about his talk with God."

The Book of Want

1

OTHER GODS

When Conchita was old enough to chew solid foods, her mother, Belén, put before her eldest daughter a cracked, blue plate holding two steaming tamales de puerco in a glistening onion-and-cilantro sauce. Her mother's cooking spoiled Conchita forever, of course. After leaving Mexico for good and settling—alone at first—in Los Angeles as a young woman of sixteen, Conchita could never find pork tamales that matched her mother's. Even when she tried to replicate the recipe, something was not quite right. But she stuck with tradition. Mornings would not be worth the trouble without tamales de puerco even if imperfectly made by her own hands. Gracias a Dios that at least Conchita could make wonderful, dark coffee—just like her mother brewed—to have with her less-than-perfect tamales. The trick was to grind a teaspoonful of sesame seeds along with the coffee beans before putting the mixture into her battered (but trustworthy) blue enamel percolator, the same one her mother had given her before she left for the United States. Now, at the age of sixty-two, Conchita missed only two things. The perfect pork tamal was one. The other was the company of a young, handsome man.

Her relatives back in Ocotlán were ashamed to admit to their neighbors that Conchita never married but, rather, had a series of novios throughout the years. They were even more embarrassed to admit that, at her age, Conchita still desired men. But why should they care? If the actor (and senior citizen) Michael Douglas could be a father with a young wife (is his wife Latina or not?), why shouldn't Conchita just *think* about sex? And look at Tony Randall. ¡Ay Dios mío! He fathered a baby when most men his age were playing with their grandchildren. And then he died of old age! At least, these were Conchita's arguments whenever her youngest sister, Julieta, scrunched up her nose in disgust when Conchita detailed precisely what she missed most about men. Conchita found Julieta's criticism extremely unfair since she had been married for almost twenty-five years and theoretically could enjoy Manuel anytime she wanted. On the other hand, Conchita had refused every offer of matrimony—and there were many—and preferred instead to experience a full variety of men without the baggage and complexities of marriage. This rule of life made sense to her. It worked, didn't it?

Granted, Conchita made one compromise last year when it came to long-term relationships. That's when she purchased a whippet at the swap meet. At first, Conchita looked for a Chihuahua but, in the end, she wanted something a little larger. The man who sold all kinds of animals at the meet said that a whippet was sort of like a large Chihuahua but with a more pleasant disposition. He even showed Conchita a well-thumbed dog book that described whippets in this way. A whippet it would be! She named him Sarkis, after an Armenian lover from long ago, a man who would have made a wonderful husband (if a woman were in the market for one), but he eventually realized that he liked men more than women. A few weeks into their dating life (twenty-five years ago during the summer of 1981 to be precise), the dashing and elegant Sarkis Avakyan announced that he was moving to Santa Barbara because he had met a wonderful person named . . . Leonard. Conchita was a bit shocked but not at all devastated; her happiness did not hang on the presence of one man. Thus, their parting was filled with love, a few tears, but no anger. Certainly, if anyone could understand the circuitous ways of the heart, it was Conchita. So, of course she would name the sleek, handsome canine after this fine man. Conchita made a mental note to drop Sarkis an e-mail about it since they were still friends and tried to keep up with each other even though he lived almost one hundred miles away.

But now, when it came to her dating life, with each passing year, men's interest in Conchita had dwindled. Though still possessing a voluptuous figure, creamy-brown skin, and large, inviting eyes, few men under the age of fifty even acknowledged her presence. And Conchita had no desire for men her own age because they looked ready for the trash heap. It was galling. If she were a famous male actor, she could have her pick of younger partners! Even if she were a more or less successful but elderly businessman, her dance card would always be full. And it was not as if Conchita did not have her rules. She never made love to married men—at least not intentionally. There was that time about fifteen years ago when she met a rather handsome man in the Dollar Tree checkout line—what was his name? Gonzalo. Yes, that was it. Gonzalo. But he lied to Conchita. Said that his wife was long dead, but, in truth, she was just visiting her sick abuela in Reseda for a week. But all this was old news. Now, as a newly retired seamstress with a nice savings account and regular Social Security checks, Conchita's bed enjoyed the warmth of only one body despite her desires to the contrary.

Ten years after Conchita left Mexico, Julieta had followed her to California when she reached the age of sixteen as well. Mónica, the middle of the three, stayed put. She would have nothing of that strange country. But Los Angeles proved a fine place to live for Conchita and Julieta. On certain streets, it felt just like Mexico. On others, it was as mean and foreign as can be. So, Conchita looked for a home in a neighborhood that teemed with brown faces like hers. Eventually, she found a nice little apartment on 15th Street just east of Ardmore Avenue, part of a duplex with its own front door and small porch, near Bishop Conaty, an all-girl high school. When Julieta came to Los Angeles, she found an equally pleasant apartment just down the street closer to Normandie Avenue, not far from Loyola High and St. Thomas the Apostle Elementary School. A good Catholic neighborhood. And even when Julieta married Manuel and wanted to buy a house, they found a comfortable two-bedroom on Hobart just a few blocks away. Manuel didn't mind staying in the same neighborhood. As long as his beautiful bride drew sustenance from Conchita's proximity, Manuel could put up with his sister-in-law's rather odd personality.

Each morning, Monday through Saturday, Julieta put on a blue or green or white velour jumpsuit, grabbed her iPod filled with "classical" music (Sinatra, Bennett, and Tormé), and did her power walk before she and Manuel had to open their camera shop for business. Now that her twin sons were living in the dorms at UCLA, she could afford to be a bit selfish with her time without feeling any guilt. Julieta had been disappointed with herself for gaining twenty-five pounds since her wedding day, but these last two years of regular exercise led to a joyous shedding of seventeen pounds with more coming off each week. Manuel couldn't keep his paws off her. These morning walks also allowed Julieta to drop in on her sister and have a cool glass of water and share a little chisme about the family back home. The hardest part of these visits was watching Conchita savor her pork tamales. But Julieta felt that much more successful with her regimen if she could finish her stopover without breaking down and having a bite.

One Saturday, Julieta power-walked up Conchita's porch, reached under the WELCOME! mat, snatched the spare key, and let herself into her sister's apartment. The delightful smell of coffee and tamales immediately overtook her and she doubted her resistance this morning.

"Hola, hermana," Julieta sang just as she pulled Sinatra out of her ears. "¡Buenos días!"

Julieta followed the delicious smells into the kitchen. Conchita stood at the window by the sink, hands on hips, staring intently at something outside. Sarkis slept curled up in his basket near the refrigerator. Julieta looked down at the table and saw a half-eaten tamal sitting in the middle of a large plate. Her mouth watered uncontrollably.

"Hermana," said Julieta as she pulled out a chair and sat down, "may I finish your tamal?"

Conchita nodded absentmindedly.

Julieta dug in and let out a moan of delight as she placed a delectable morsel of tamal onto her tongue. A little treat wouldn't ruin her recent weight loss. Julieta then grabbed the percolator and refilled Conchita's coffee cup.

"May I finish your coffee, too?" she asked as she scooped two spoonfuls of sugar into the cup.

"Sí," Conchita whispered.

Julieta sipped the coffee for a few moments. Conchita didn't move from the window.

"¿Qué pasó?" Julieta finally asked.

"Look," said Conchita.

Julieta sighed at having to leave her feast. Nonetheless, she stood—coffee cup in hand—and joined her sister at the window.

"What am I looking at?" she asked as she took another sip.

Conchita pointed. "¿No ves?"

Julieta squinted. She never wore glasses on her power walks because she hated how they would slide down her nose the second she broke a sweat.

"Him," Conchita sighed. "Don't you see him?"

Julieta thought she could discern a figure but she wasn't certain. And she couldn't remember which neighbor lived on that side. She went back to the table to finish the tamal.

"Well?" said Conchita.

"What's so interesting about your neighbor?"

"Why is he sitting Indian style on his lawn?"

Julieta shrugged and took another sip of coffee.

Conchita thought for a moment. "Actually, it's not quite Indian style. Not the kind of Indian like from here."

"What are you talking about?"

"He's sitting like that statue you have in your garden."

Julieta laughed. "Like the Buddha?"

"¡Sí!" exclaimed Conchita. "Él se sienta como el Buddha."

Julieta responded by taking a sip of coffee.

"And he looks different, doesn't he?" Conchita added.

Julieta sighed. She didn't want to admit that she hadn't really seen on whom her sister was spying. So, Julieta offered a noncommittal response: "Does he?"

"Sí."

"How?"

Conchita turned to her sister and thought for a moment. "Younger," she finally said.

Julieta couldn't play dumb anymore. "Hermana, who are we talking about?"

Conchita shook her head. "Where are your glasses?"

Julieta blushed. "At home."

"Mr. Rojo is who I'm talking about," said Conchita as she came to the table. "My neighbor," she added as she sat.

"I know he's your neighbor," Julieta said. And then, after a little thought: "Botox?"

"No! Not Mr. Rojo. That's plain silly."

"Why do you call him 'Mr.'?" said Julieta as she scraped the last bit of tamal onto her fork. "Don't you know his first name?"

Conchita hesitated. "His name is Moisés."

They sat in silence for a minute.

"His wife's been dead for over a year," Julieta finally said. "¿No?"

Conchita grimaced. "¿Y qué?"

"You have a crush on him?"

"Don't be tonta!"

Julieta leaned close to her sister. "He's a widower," she reminded Conchita. "And he's about your age, maybe a little older, yes, but close enough."

Conchita narrowed her eyes. "That power walking has shrunk your brain along with your nalgas."

"I was just saying . . . "

Conchita rose to her feet so fast her chair almost fell over. She crossed her arms and glared at her sister. "¡Ya basta!"

"Okay, okay," said Julieta. She looked at her watch. "Oh, I have to go! Manny will be mad if I'm late."

The moment Julieta left, Conchita went back to the kitchen window. Mr. Rojo still sat in his backyard, straight-backed and cross-legged on a blue blanket, eyes closed, hands resting palm side up on his knees. Conchita shook her head.

"Tonta," she murmured. "My sister is tonta."

◪

The feeble air-conditioning unit in Conchita's bedroom window rattled and hummed. Normally these sounds blended into an innocuous white noise that lulled Conchita to sleep on hot L.A. nights. But not tonight. This night, the air conditioner supplied a harsh soundtrack as Conchita fell in and out of disquieting dreams. Faces and voices came at her from all directions. Julieta, Manuel, Mónica, and even her late mother, Belén. Their lips moved fast as cats as they scolded Conchita, told her to stop being a puta, find a man, and settle down *¡finalmente!* But she told them she wasn't a whore . . . she never accepted money for her lovers' company. She liked being with a nice variety of healthy men, that's all! But their lips moved faster and faster, their entreaties taking on the ugly rattle and hum of the air conditioner.

Conchita finally woke and sat up, her nightgown soaked through. She stood and stripped the wet garment off as fast as she could. If Conchita kept the lights off, she could walk naked to the kitchen without fear of anyone seeing her through the sheer curtains that adorned all the windows of her apartment. But now, an almost-full moon would illuminate her trek. She needed to find something cool and refreshing from the refrigerator. Perhaps some mango juice would help. Or maybe a Jarritos grapefruit soda. As she navigated through the shadows, Conchita admired how the moonlight danced and shimmered on her wet skin. This was a beautiful body that looked twenty years younger than it was! A body that deserved to be touched and enjoyed by a virile, potent man. Conchita almost hoped that some handsome, youngish insomniac would be walking his dog just then so that he could catch a glimpse of this daring, mature woman as she paraded about in the outfit God had designed for her in His infinite wisdom.

Conchita reached the kitchen and opened the refrigerator's door but a crack. Sarkis stirred in his basket but settled back into a beautiful canine slumber. She opened the door wider but had forgotten how bright the automatic light was. Conchita wasn't *that* daring. She preferred not to be lit up like a singer on a stage. So she closed the refrigerator door a bit so that her hand could fit. Making a last-minute decision not to drink soda at this hour, Conchita quickly snatched a bottle of mango juice from the top shelf and just as quickly closed the refrigerator. She opened the bottle and drank deeply. Quenched for the moment, Conchita moved the cold, wet bottle down the side of her right breast, along her ribs, and then in toward her smooth belly. She shivered. And then Conchita heard it. Her eyes flitted back and forth and she held her breath. What was that sound? The air conditioner unit in the bedroom? No. This was human. A hum. A moan. No! It was something in between a hum and a moan. Conchita put the bottle down and crept to the window, following the noise. She stayed low because the sink and half the counter were awash in moonlight. The little hairs on the back of her neck stood on end as she approached the sound.

Slowly, Conchita moved her face to the open window. And what she saw sent a chill down her spine. Mr. Rojo sat as he had earlier that day, but this time he emitted a rhythmic noise, deep from within his chest. The moon illuminated him and the blue blanket he sat on; had he been there all day? And what was he doing? Though Conchita's mind filled with questions, she grew calmer. Something about the noise made by this man quieted her, composed her. And she noticed that Mr. Rojo looked exquisite sitting there in the moonlight, lost in the cadence of his mysterious chant. Exquisite? Such silliness! Mr. Rojo and his late wife had lived next door for almost ten years and not once had Conchita entertained such thoughts. But what had transformed him? His wife's death? No. That made no sense. Even to Conchita, it was clear that Mr. Rojo had loved Carmela with all his heart. Surely he should have aged faster when she died. But there he sat, looking younger, trimmer, and almost radiant with renewed heartiness.

In her reverie, Conchita let out a deep, longing sigh. She wanted the peace Mr. Rojo now enjoyed. And the more she thought about it, the more she realized that she wanted Mr. Rojo, too. Conchita blinked, shook her head, and tried to chase away such notions. But her eyes traveled back to this man. So immobile. Where did such stillness come from? But wait! He moved! Conchita squinted even though she had perfect vision, unlike her sister. She watched as Mr. Rojo's body shifted and quivered just a bit. And then Conchita's mouth fell open. Could it be? Her eyes flickered as a shadow grew beneath Mr. Rojo because his body gradually rose, first an inch, then two, then three. Conchita held her breath. And then Mr. Rojo stopped rising and hovered about a foot above the blanket. At that moment, Conchita realized that Mr. Rojo was the most beautiful man she had ever seen. And it was also at that moment that Conchita knew, without misgiving, where her life would take her: to this singular man.

Conchita watched Mr. Rojo for two hours. She stood, naked and bathed in the moonlight, loving this man who could defy gravity. Her whippet slept peacefully in his basket, unaware of his mistress's presence. Eventually Conchita's eyes began to tire and the thought of her soft bed kept intruding on her thoughts. She sighed, took one last look at Mr. Rojo, reached down to pat Sarkis's sleek brow, and went to bed. Her feet took her away as if she had no choice in the matter.

The next morning, Conchita woke feeling refreshed despite getting no more than a few hours of sleep. It was Sunday, so her sister would not be dropping in. Conchita could enjoy her solitude with nothing more than her dog, the

newspaper, breakfast, and the memory of last night. She put on a robe, slid
her feet into slippers, and went to get the paper. As she opened the door, the
morning's cool air enveloped her face; she took a deep breath. What a perfect
day! Conchita opened her eyes and looked at the sidewalk. She let out a little
laugh. The newspaper had landed so that it stood perfectly balanced on one end,
looking like a bizarre, newsprint plant growing out of the cement. As she picked
it up, she looked to her right and saw the paperboy bicycle away and then toss
another newspaper two houses down, which landed with a *plop!* into the middle
of a large puddle at the base of an avocado tree. Conchita laughed again but then
shot a glance at Mr. Rojo's house. Had he slept? she wondered. Did he stay out
all night? Did he float all night? Was it called "floating"?

The morning's chill dissipated in due course. By lunchtime, the
thermometer reached ninety degrees and the humidity stood at ten percent.
But, other than to take Sarkis out for two walks, Conchita spent the day inside
despite this, her favorite weather. Normally, she reveled in such heat. This was
the kind of day Conchita waited for so she could squeeze into one of her four
floral sundresses, slip on a pair of green, open-toed, kitten-heeled slingbacks,
and rub a drop or two of baby oil on her ample cleavage until that still-perfect
brown expanse glistened like a well-marinated roast. Once prepared for the
L.A. sun, Conchita would stride out of her apartment, catch the bus at Pico
and Ardmore, and head downtown for a day of window-shopping, which, as
she well understood, was a mere excuse for showing off her body to those who
could appreciate it. But in recent years, all the whistles and offers of romance
came from the old men, those viejitos who congregated at the innumerable
narrow Mexican food counters that lined the first floors of the aging office
buildings in the old part of downtown. This disappointment, however, wasn't
what kept Conchita at home this day. No. This day was new, different. Because
last night she had witnessed a most remarkable event. Not a miracle. Not like
her tonta friend Amalia Gómez who a decade ago told Conchita in a breathless
announcement that she had seen a crucifix in the sky and that this could only be
un milagro—a true miracle and sign from God. Conchita was not as foolish as
Amalia.

No. Last night's event—yes, "event" was the word Conchita decided upon—
had a basis in science, not some supernatural intercession. She remembered
watching on the Discovery Channel with rapt fascination a documentary
about an Israeli gentleman who utilized his mind, and nothing more, to bend
spoons, forks, and knives. Remarkable. But not a miracle. Something to do with
natural magnetic forces that surround us every day though only a few know

how to harness them. So, if a man could twist cutlery into pretzels by merely concentrating, certainly Mr. Rojo—Moisés—could rise above his blanket for a few hours without breaking the laws of physics or relying on other gods. No. ¡No! Not a miracle. A normal event purely of this world. Based on science. Nothing more. Nothing less.

But what to do to get into Moisés's life? Knock on his door unannounced? Conchita pondered what her approach should be. Normally, the man made the first move after she had prepared the way with her charm and beauty. At least that's how it happened when she was a bit younger. Conchita realized that Moisés was different from most men. Someone with such remarkable powers had to be considered by special rules.

Lost in such thoughts, the day slipped away. Before she knew it, it was seven o'clock, the sun was setting, and Conchita had done nothing more than take Sarkis out for two short walks. She barely ate anything all day and could not imagine eating a full dinner. So, she forced herself to eat a piece of pan dulce with a cup of coffee. She was sticky from the heat. A bath, that's what Conchita needed. The bathtub was a perfect place for her to think a bit more about her neighbor while she soaked in apricot-scented bubbles and shaved her legs.

After Conchita was clean, smooth, perfumed, and dressed, she had a thought. She could knock on Moisés's door with the pretense of needing assistance of some sort. Oh, such silliness. She was acting like a teenager.

Conchita looked about her dark apartment. Light. She needed light so that she could think. Conchita moved from lamp to lamp, illuminating each corner and scanning her neat surroundings like a shipwrecked wretch in search of sustenance. As she reached the last lamp, Conchita found that the bulb had burned out. So annoying. She had just replaced it last week. But wait! That's it! She could pretend that it was something more. A dead lamp that only a man such as Moisés could bring to life. Conchita would walk herself next door and feign helplessness with all things mechanical and Moisés, being a true gentleman, would surely offer to have a look at the lamp. When he discovers that it's nothing more than a lifeless bulb, she will thank him profusely, apologize for being such a silly woman, and offer him dinner for his kindness. Yes! So perfect. So simple. True, this amounted to playing games, something Conchita tried to avoid. So, she promised herself: this one time only, that's it. If her ploy failed, so be it. Conchita would get on with her life. She had never been desperate, and she was not going to begin now.

Conchita scampered like a young girl into the bathroom to take one more look at herself before beginning her adventure. Not so bad for sixty-two! Good skin. Generous curves. And those eyes! She left her apartment with great hope and clicked over to Moisés's front door. Conchita straightened her already straight sundress, coughed, and then knocked softly. Silence. She knocked again, this time a bit harder. Silence again. Conchita stood there for two minutes, mind rushing, wondering what to do next. Where could he be? Did he go out for dinner? With a woman? Was she silly in assuming that this fine-looking man had not already been snatched up by someone else? Someone younger? And prettier? It was too much to take. Conchita turned quickly and went back to her apartment.

She called Julieta's house but Manuel answered.

"Hola, Manny. Is Julieta there?"

Manny sounded winded, a little bothered. "She went out. Shopping."

Conchita thought for a moment. "Does she have her cell on her?"

"No. It's sitting here on the desk."

"Oh, well . . . "

Manuel interrupted: "Conchita, I need to get off. I'll let her know you called."

She put the receiver back down in its cradle. It was best that Julieta wasn't in. Conchita would sound like a fool if she told her about everything that had happened the last two days. She sat down in front of the TV and looked for something to take her mind off of Moisés. Sarkis padded into the room, stared at his mistress, and decided to go back to his basket in the kitchen. Too damn hot. Conchita switched from channel to channel. Nothing. So many choices and so little to watch. Conchita finally settled on an old Angelines Fernández movie. She was Spanish, not Mexican. ¿No? But she made it *big* in Mexico. At least that's what Conchita remembered. Didn't she die about ten years ago? Oh, no matter. At least Conchita could concentrate on something. But instead of being a diversion, the film merely acted as a sedative. Within minutes, Conchita's head had fallen back and she snored softly as the movie continued, came to an end, and several other programs started and finished.

She finally woke to an infomercial about an exercise device that looked like something designed to torture prisoners of war. Conchita blinked as the muscular man and woman flashed huge, perfectly aligned white teeth and swore that their astonishing physiques could be had by anyone who used the device for ten minutes a day—without dieting!—for a mere $29.99 per month for eleven months. She blinked again and then realized that the sun was down and the moon suffused her apartment with a bright glow. Conchita flicked off the TV and sat on the couch feeling empty, defeated. And why hadn't Julieta called back? So annoying. But then she heard it. That same chant from the night before. She jumped up, suddenly energized, and ran to the kitchen window. Tonight, there was a slight breeze, which made the curtain billow in just a bit. And there he was: Moisés sitting like the Buddha, not yet floating, eyes closed, chanting in utter, idyllic peace.

Conchita looked at the oven's digital clock: exactly midnight. She turned back to Moisés just in time. He started to quiver again, just like last night. Within a few moments, he hovered an inch or two above the blanket. He rose slowly and with each inch, Conchita's heart beat faster. Possibly this *was* a miracle. Perhaps in his grief at the loss of his beloved wife, Moisés had crossed the threshold into some kind of sainthood. Imagine! To live next door to un santo. But did saints go out on dates? Did they make love to beautiful, full-bodied, mature women? Oh, this could be bad. No. He was no saint. Merely a man who had mastered an ancient discipline. A man who used science to levitate—yes, that's the word—levitate himself a foot above the ground. This was quite real, very much of this world.

Conchita knew that she must act. She ran her fingers through her hair, straightened her dress, and thought about how she could get into Moisés's backyard. Because her neighbor didn't have a dog, Conchita assumed that his side gate wouldn't be locked. Filled with resolve, she marched out of the kitchen, into her small living room, through the foyer, and outside. The moon was now full and glorious in its intensity. Conchita walked down her cement steps and onto the sidewalk. The street was empty as the neighborhood slept in preparation for the work and school week to begin. She approached Moisés's gate and . . . yes! No lock. She opened it slowly just in case it squeaked, but it did not. Conchita entered and walked carefully by the side of the house. The moon's rays were obstructed and she didn't want to crash down on whatever Moisés might store in that narrow area. But her path proved to be clear and she reached the end of the house and walked out into the backyard.

Conchita approached Moisés, treading tentatively, one foot in front of the other, as if she were walking a tightrope. He did not notice the intruder; he floated above the ground, his chanting uninterrupted. And then it happened. Conchita hadn't noticed it before but Moisés was now two feet in the air and was still rising, slowly, yes, but rising nonetheless. How much higher would he—*could* he—go? Conchita stood not more than ten feet away. And Moisés kept on rising. Conchita looked around, frantic. What if he didn't stop? Was there a rope she could throw to save him from going up beyond the treetops, telephone poles, clouds? She couldn't find a rope but there was a hose. No. That wouldn't work. Too awkward. She moved closer, giving up her search for a lifeline. Now Moisés floated almost five feet above his blue blanket. Conchita took a deep breath and strode right up to him, her nose almost touching his left knee.

"Mr. Rojo," she said, softly. And then she drew up inner strength to use his first name: "Moisés," she said. "Stop this."

Moisés opened his eyes and blinked. He looked down at Conchita, not with surprise, but with a small smile. She smiled back at this beautiful, strange man. Moisés removed his left hand from his knee and held it out to Conchita. And she took it. Gently, tentatively, not a tight grasp. His hand felt warm, dry, safe. Conchita breathed deeply and—what was that? A glorious, almost overwhelming scent of roses! But Moisés's backyard was filled with lemon trees, not a rose in sight. No matter. The scent filled Conchita with a serenity she had never known as an adult. She closed her eyes and inhaled deeply. Her smile grew broader.

And then suddenly, after a few moments, her feet began to slip out of her slingbacks. At first Conchita flinched, opened her eyes, and thought of trying to keep her shoes from falling off but she gave up. It didn't matter. Because she held the hand of a saint who cared enough—who loved her enough—to reach out and share his miracle with her. As they rose higher, Moisés's chanting brought Conchita such joy that her eyes filled with tears. She could hear a dog bark from another yard far below her. A pigeon flew by, barely noticing them. Her shoes fell from her feet, first the left one, then the right, and landed softly on Moisés's blue blanket. Conchita tried to blink away her tears. The moon shone brightly, illuminating Moisés's perfect, smiling face. And Conchita knew she was exactly where she belonged.

2

HAS HE BEEN THERE FOR YOU?

"Hola, Manny," said Conchita. "Is Julieta there?"

Manuel clutched the receiver and breathed deeply through his mouth. Esta mujer, he thought as he shook his head. "She went out," he finally answered. "Shopping."

"Does she have her cell on her?"

"No," said Manuel as he looked around. "It's sitting here on the desk."

"Oh, well . . . "

Manuel interrupted: "Conchita, I need to get off. I'll let her know you called."

He dropped the receiver in its cradle with a loud *clack!* not waiting for a response from his sister-in-law. Manuel let out a little laugh when he realized that he actually hadn't lied to Conchita. Julieta was, indeed, shopping in downtown and she had left her cell phone here on the desk. He had been lying so often lately that his truthfulness with Conchita amused him.

Manuel grabbed his wallet and keys. He had told Julieta that he was going to get together with his compadre, Tomás, and would be home pretty late. Tomás lived way out in Long Beach and was long divorced from Elena who moved to Las Vegas five years ago. They never had any children. So Tomás became the perfect alibi for Manuel because Julieta had no connections with him. Manuel walked to the door, his heart beating hard. He was actually going through with it. He never thought that he'd have the huevos to do this. But the date was made and he'd better get going so that he wouldn't be late.

As he reached for the doorknob, he caught his reflection in the ornate mirror by the coatrack. Conchita had given that mirror to Manuel and Julieta as a wedding gift. Handcrafted in Mexico, Julieta loved that mirror because it reminded her of home. Manuel hated it upon first sight. Too fancy for his taste.

It was a heavy, beveled, oval monolith with Moorish swirls etched around its edges and glass flowers glued haphazardly—to his thinking—at the narrow ends of the mirror. But it served its purpose. And at that moment, its purpose was to reassure Manuel that he still possessed handsome, sharp features and a full head of hair, though now graying on top and at his temples. He had agonized over the blue striped shirt but now, as he posed in front of the mirror he hated, Manuel acknowledged that the garment draped nicely over his still-muscular torso and made his midsection look trimmer while accentuating his broad shoulders. He was as ready as he'd ever be.

As he eased his Lexus onto the Santa Monica Freeway, Manuel tried to concentrate on his breathing. Breathe in, breathe out, breathe in, breathe out. Calm down, he thought. He licked his dry lips and tried to swallow but it almost hurt as he gulped too much air. Breathe in, breathe out, breathe in, breathe out. Why all this traffic? On Sunday night, who else is heading in this direction? Traffic had become so unpredictable these last five or six years that Manuel wondered if it were time to get out of L.A. Maybe Oxnard or perhaps Bakersfield. But he knew even those cities now choked with congestion. It all annoyed him. People annoyed him. Too many bodies living and driving and just being in the way.

Manuel drove west as the sun set. So stunning, even though he knew that smog made the reds and purples more brilliant. The traffic eventually tapered off so that Manuel could now sustain a less frustrating speed. Where's that exit? Ah! Lincoln. He got off and eventually turned left on Pico Boulevard. Funny. He was now near the beach, no more than a mile away, and he drove on the same street that ran close to his own home. But this part of Pico was a dozen miles west in Santa Monica. Within moments, Manuel found the right apartment complex and turned down the alley, as she had suggested, to find a place to park. At first glance, the building looked shiny and new, but as he walked along the sidewalk toward the entrance, he noticed that the stucco had been patched in many spots and gang tags had been halfheartedly covered with a tan paint that was one shade lighter than the rest of the building.

Manuel approached the large front doors. They were of glass, so he could look into the lobby. She had told him to buzz apartment 8. He shivered; he had forgotten that Santa Monica could be a good fifteen to twenty degrees cooler than his part of town. Manuel wished he had brought a jacket. He pulled out his reading glasses and searched for number 8. He found it next to a wrinkled slip of paper that had *C. Muñoz* printed in pencil. He pushed the button and waited. Manual took a deep breath and wondered if he should turn and go but the intercom crackled and a small voice came out: "Manny?"

"Yes."

"Second floor," she said. "Take the stairs. The elevator takes too long."

More silence. Then a sickly buzz. Manuel pushed the right door and it opened with a metal creak. He entered the lobby and was immediately overcome with the scent of Pine-Sol. The brown and gold floor tile gleamed, freshly mopped. He slowly walked to the stairs so as not to slip. As Manuel trudged up to the main hallway, each step felt heavy. Manuel smelled pizza and pork chops. His stomach growled and he realized that he had not eaten dinner. No matter. He found apartment 8 and knocked. Again he waited. What was wrong with her? Why did she do that? To annoy him? And then the door opened just a crack revealing one large, brown eye and a nose.

"It's me," said Manuel, realizing how silly this sounded.

The door opened wider and there she stood. Manuel exhaled loudly. It was Carmen, all right. Same face, only a little broader, as was her body. And instead of the long, black hair she wore as a girl, she now had it closely cropped and tight around her face, which, to Manuel's thinking, was appropriate for her age. Long hair is for the young, he thought. She looks good.

"Come in," Carmen said in almost a whisper.

She moved to the side to let Manuel pass. As he entered, Manuel noticed for the first time that Carmen wore white hospital scrubs with little cartoon farm animals stenciled throughout the cotton fabric.

"Sit," she said, as she motioned to a green couch.

"Nice outfit."

Carmen laughed. "Just got home from a double shift."

"Nothing wrong with a little hard work."

"Do you want a drink?"

"Sure," said Manuel. He maneuvered around the coffee table and sat down. "Whatever you got."

Carmen walked to the small kitchen, which opened to the rest of the apartment. Manuel scanned the room. Carmen kept it neat and in order except for the walls, which she had covered with colorful Mexican masks. Manuel recognized several that were used in traditional dances. There was La Borracha— the drunken woman—worn in the Torito dance. And there hung three wrinkled faces—viejitos—for the dance of the old men, one of Manuel's favorites. He remembered how his older sister's folkloric dance troupe did them all, dances from Michoacán to Guanajuato to Jalisco to Oaxaca. When he was nine, Manuel marveled as Ernestine kept up with the other girls and boys who were two and three years older than she. But she always became the crowd's favorite. Manuel remembered how Ernestine would bat her fake eyelashes and offer a gleaming smile as she proudly danced in bright outfits. A week after Manuel turned eleven, the dance troupe joined his family in church to pray that Ernestine's young soul would soon be with Jesús, La Virgen, y todos los santos.

"Beer?"

Manuel looked up and blinked.

"Samuel Adams?" she clarified.

"What?"

Carmen held it up as if to prove she wasn't lying. "See, Manny. It's Samuel Adams."

"Yes, gracias, that's perfect."

She grabbed another beer, popped the tops, and walked to the coffee table. Carmen handed one to Manuel, who nodded his thanks. She stood for a moment pondering where to sit. She finally decided on a large stuffed armchair across from Manuel. Carmen sat and held up the beer.

"To us," she said with a small smile.

Manuel didn't move. Carmen sighed. Manuel took a long swig of his beer. Carmen put hers down on the coffee table without taking a drink.

"Sorry," said Carmen.

"I like your masks."

Carmen smiled. "Yes, I've been collecting them since . . . "

And then Manuel remembered. He had given Carmen a diablo mask as a present before she left for El Paso, where her father had decided to move the whole family. It was their little joke: Carmen liked to call Manuel her little devil. They were both seventeen when she left. Manuel suddenly turned his head and started searching for the devil mask. Carmen stood and walked to the far wall by a large window. She reached up and lifted a battered, grinning face from its nail.

"Here it is," said Carmen.

Manuel jumped up and almost ran to her. He reached for the mask, took it from Carmen's hand, and held it up.

"Goddamn!" was all he could say. "Goddamn!"

Carmen laughed.

"Thirty years," he added.

"Thirty-five," Carmen corrected.

Manuel turned the mask this way and that. "How did we get so old?"

"Who's old?" Carmen laughed. "I don't know about you but I'm still breathing," she added with a pat of Manuel's arm.

Manuel handed the mask back to Carmen, walked quickly to the couch, and sat down. She re-hung the mask and went back to her chair.

After a few moments, Manuel said gently, "So, a nurse, huh?"

"Yes."

"Like it?"

"Oh, it's a job." Carmen shifted in her chair. "But I have a lot of freedom with my schedule." And I like working on the pediatrics floor."

"How long have you been back in L.A.?"

Carmen turned away and looked at the devil mask. "A while."

"How long is 'a while'?"

She turned back to Manuel. "Almost twenty."

"Months?"

"Years."

Manuel's mouth opened just a bit, frozen, a response stuck below his tongue. Finally: "¿Cómo puede ser la verdad?"

"It *is* true."

"And you haven't bothered to contact me until now?"

At that moment, Manuel realized that perspiration covered his face. He wiped his forehead and upper lip with his palm and he tried to control his breathing. Manuel needed to understand, but he felt himself falling someplace, somewhere he didn't know.

"I assumed you were married," said Carmen.

Manuel understood. Of course he had married. How could he not? Manuel had assumed the same of Carmen, particularly when she stopped writing back and his letters were returned from El Paso as undeliverable. He had kept Carmen's letters—a baker's dozen—wrapped in a small, clean piece of blue gabardine that he'd cut from the back of one of his old suits that no longer fit his fast-growing, seventeen-year-old frame. This soft packet of sweet, childish writing sat at the bottom of a battered Hush Puppies box hidden safely in Manuel's cluttered closet, a place Julieta never dared enter. But now here she sat, his high school lover, thirty-five years older than the last day he'd seen her. A nurse with a small but neat rent-controlled apartment in Santa Monica. And they had planned this meeting two weeks ago, the result of a long e-mail she'd sent to Manuel through a link from his camera shop's Web site. Carmen had told him that she lived not too far away and that she was the mother of a girl—no, a woman—named Teresa. A woman who, she'd said, was their daughter. But in everything Carmen had revealed in that e-mail, Manuel realized that she had never indicated how long she'd been back.

"May I see it?" said Manuel.

Carmen stood and walked to a large bookcase near a door that Manuel assumed led to the bedroom. She reached for a small, wooden box, lifted its lid, and pulled out an envelope. She closed the box but didn't move; it seemed to Manuel that Carmen was reconsidering this part of the visit.

"May I?" said Manuel, trying unsuccessfully to control his voice. It quavered a bit. He coughed in an attempt to regain control of himself.

Carmen finally came back to Manuel and held the envelope out to him. He took it and turned it over once and then twice. The envelope had a postmark of almost a month ago. Carmen's name and address were in a careful, almost childlike hand. The return address said Teresa Muñoz—W86910, which was followed by a post office box number in Chowchilla, California.

"What's this?" Manuel asked, pointing to the W86910.

"Her prison number," she answered.

Manuel let out a sigh. Of course it was. His eyes returned to the envelope. At the left corner, stamped in large, red, block letters, were the words:

CENTRAL CALIFORNIA WOMEN'S FACILITY STATE PRISON

Carmen sat and took a slow, long drink from her beer. Manuel opened the envelope and pulled out several sheets of neatly folded, lined yellow paper.

"Turn to the last page," said Carmen. "The last two paragraphs."

Manuel thumbed through the pages, all of which were filled from top to bottom with the same neat handwriting that adorned the front of the envelope. When he reached the last page, he read to himself:

Amá, I met with my counselor after lunch. She told me if I was working, my release date would be moved to October 1 instead of next year. So I asked about the work furlough that they got to offer and they let me sign up. This is better than parole because I get out sooner. "Over the wall" my friend La Queenie calls it. She's tough but she's been good for me. She makes me think. I asked La Queenie if she still prayed. She said yeah she still prayed but she wondered if God listened. I told her God has been there for me even with me being locked up in here. Amá, has he been there for you? I hope so.

Manuel took a long breath and blinked.

"Are you okay?" Carmen asked.

Manuel nodded. He returned to the letter:

So, Amá, I've been thinking about what we talked about. And I've decided. When I get out of here on furlough, I do want to meet him. I think I need to. I mentioned this to La Queenie and she said that every girl should know her father. La Queenie never knew hers. She said she wished all the time that she knew where he was. So, I know my father is down there in L.A. like you told me, finally. I wish you had told me when I was little. Maybe I wouldn't be here if I knew about him when I was a girl. But I'm not mad at you, Amá. I just want to see him. Please ask him, Amá. Te amo mucho. Tu hija, Teresa.

Manuel blinked hard and reread the last paragraph. He looked up at Carmen, who sat at the edge of her chair.

"It's up to you," she said.

"Por supuesto."

"But I felt that I had to let you know."

Manuel rearranged the pages, folded them carefully, and put the letter back in the envelope. He stood and handed it to Carmen.

"Julieta doesn't know about you or her," he said.

Carmen put the letter on her lap but kept it tightly in her grip.

"Can you imagine," continued Manuel, "if I told her?"

"I don't know Julieta," she said, barely moving her lips. "Maybe she'd be okay with it."

"You're right," he said. "You don't know her."

"But maybe she'd understand," she kept on. "We were young. You didn't even know Julieta yet."

Manuel stood and walked to the door. "No," he said. "No."

Carmen quickly got to her feet and followed Manuel. "But I thought that you would."

"No."

"But why did you bother to come here?"

Manuel grabbed the doorknob without turning it. "I don't know," he said.

"Look," said Carmen, "you don't have to decide now. Right? Think about it. Please, Manny. Just think about it."

Manuel looked at Carmen and tried to smile. And then he simply opened the door and left. As Manuel escaped the lobby and was safely out of the building, he walked briskly to his Lexus. He started the car and decided to skip the freeway and take Pico Boulevard all the way home. Manuel needed to digest what had just happened. As he drove, Teresa's careful handwriting appeared everywhere he looked. He shook his head and tried to concentrate on his dialogue with Carmen. Manuel's imagination softened his response, modified the scene. But reality kept taking over and what had actually happened in that apartment could not be denied. And like a pendejo, he'd walked into it. Just based on the e-mail, Manuel knew what Carmen would ask. So, why did he go? He could have avoided this all. But what did Carmen think? Thirty-five years of ignorance is too long to wipe away with one visit. It wouldn't help anyone. Not Teresa, not Carmen, and certainly not Julieta. Julieta. What would she do if she knew about this visit? How would she react to Teresa? No. It was too much to ask of him. Teresa was no child. She was a grown woman who was serving time in a "women's facility." What a phrase. Women's facility. It's a prison. And Manuel was not to blame for it.

Manuel drove in a shroud of images and words and too many emotions to decipher. He drove the twelve miles without thinking about the act of driving. Manuel finally pulled into his driveway and saw that Julieta's car·sat in the garage. He entered through the kitchen. The house was dark except for a light emanating from the bedroom.

"Julieta," he called.

"In here!"

Julieta was in the bedroom posing in front of the long mirror on the closet door. Price tags bounced up and down as she admired her new skirt and blouse. Manuel stopped at the doorway and looked at his wife.

"You're home early," she said as she kept her eyes on the mirror.

"Tomás wasn't feeling too well so we called it a night after one beer."

Julieta turned around slowly with her arms held out as if she were about to fly.

"And your sister called before I went out," he added.

"You like?"

"What?"

"My new outfit."

Manuel walked up to Julieta and grabbed her hands.

"Beautiful," he said.

Julieta gave Manuel a broad grin. "Really?"

"Sí, mi amor," said Manuel as he brought Julieta close to him.

"Not bad for a fifty-something-year-old woman?"

"Perfect."

"The truth?" she asked, letting out a little laugh.

"Sí," he said as he pulled her in tighter. "Es la verdad."

3

DOMINGO

Julieta nudged Manuel with her elbow. He offered nothing more than a grunt in response and pulled the blankets over his head.

"Please come with me," she said. "Like we used to before the twins."

Manuel mumbled something.

"What, mi cielo?"

Manuel lifted his head an inch from the pillow: "That was almost nineteen years ago."

"So?"

He let his head drop dramatically onto the pillow and pulled the blankets tighter around his face. Julieta nudged him again.

"I'm asleep," said Manuel. "Snore," he added dramatically.

Julieta stood and walked to the dresser. Manuel peeked out from beneath the blankets, sighed, and sat up.

"Mi amor," he began, "I work six days a week at that camera store. I deserve to sleep late on Sunday, don't I?"

Julieta turned. "It's my store, too, and I'm right there working by your side those same six days."

"I know, I know," he said.

"Not to mention doing our taxes and keeping inventory."

"I know you work hard too," said Manuel, holding up his hands in surrender. "That's not what I meant, mi amor."

"What did you mean?"

"El domingo es mi día favorito."

"Sunday is my favorite day, too," she said in almost a whisper.

Manuel was at a loss. No matter what he said, he was going to lose this one. He listened to the noises outside: the Sunday *Times* landing with a thump in their driveway, a few rambunctious dogs yapping, giddy birds chirping to their hearts' content.

"So, you're going to see Tomás tonight?" Julieta finally said.

"Yes," said Manuel. He paused for a moment before adding: "Tomás is feeling kind of down. Sunday is when he really feels like a lonely, old man."

"He's our age," she said. "And if he tried, he could meet someone nice and marry again."

"People don't change," Manuel responded. "From the moment you're born until the day you leave this earth, you're basically the same person."

Julieta ignored this last comment. She simply came back to bed and sat at the edge of the mattress. Manuel admired her figure. The power walking had helped Julieta drop a lot of weight that she'd slowly accumulated during motherhood. Manuel pondered whether he could seduce her into missing morning Mass. He caressed her arm.

"Have a little communion with me," he smiled.

Julieta let out a tiny laugh and stood up.

"I get the body of Christ only once a week," she said as she walked to the bathroom. "I can get the body of Manny every day, if I want it."

Manuel scratched his chin and coughed. Julieta started to brush her teeth. After a few moments, she swished her mouth and spat into the sink. She grimaced to examine her teeth in the mirror. Perfect. Never a cavity, no need for braces. By this age, Julieta's mother and father had lost most of their teeth and both wore annoying sets of dentures. She came back to the bedroom because Manuel had been so quiet. There he sat in bed, the man she'd loved for almost three decades.

"Well, say hello to God for me," he said.

Julieta nodded and went back to the bathroom to finish getting ready for Mass. Manuel slid down and buried his face in the pillow. He was asleep within minutes.

❑

As she drove to church, Julieta wondered why she drew such comfort from this Catholic ritual. Perhaps it reminded her of her childhood in Mexico. But that couldn't be it. Weekly Mass was never a big part of her life despite the fact that their pueblo possessed a beautiful basilica. Even gringos made pilgrimages to this holy place, pale men and women who wept silently as they absorbed the power and beauty of the church's architecture and consecrated statues. But even with this wonderful house of worship in their midst, Belén repeatedly told Julieta and her two sisters that there was no need to attend Mass each Sunday because

God was everywhere. This raised grave concerns in the mind of the young Julieta. Was God there when she went pee-pee in the cold, stinky outhouse? And was God there when her parents made funny noises in their bedroom late at night when they thought the children were asleep? Julieta now laughed at such childish logic. As a long-married woman and the mother of twin boys, she understood the kind of love that rose above the most ridiculous and messy of human activities.

Julieta came to a red light and stopped behind an old Buick. She and Manual had treated themselves to matching Lexus sedans two years ago, identical except in color: Cypress Gold Metallic for her, Cypress Pearl for him. They'd worked hard putting extra time into the camera shop and finally paying off their mortgage. After too many years of driving used cars, she and Manuel believed they'd earned the right to pamper themselves. The twins happily took the old Corollas off their parents' hands. Didn't she and Manny deserve a little luxury? Of course they did.

Julieta soon hit Pico Boulevard and turned right. She could already tell that it was going to be a hot day. She flicked on the air conditioning and started to search for a place to park. This used to be a simple task ten or even five years ago. But with time came more cars, less room. Last Sunday, Julieta had to go around the block twice to find a spot, which put her in a very un-Christian mood. She passed the front of the church, already teeming with adults, teenagers, and young children making their way through the front doors. Julieta reached the corner and turned right on Mariposa Street. She eased past the rectory keeping one eye in front of her and the other at the curb hoping for a vacancy. But no luck. Too many damn cars! Maybe she should walk to Mass from now on. But on days like today, she'd enter the church a wilted flower. Or perhaps she could make it to the 6:30 a.m. Mass. Surely few people got up that early, thus leaving the streets absolutely screaming with open spaces for her Lexus. She quickly shook that idea from her head. The best Julieta could do on a Sunday was 8:00 a.m. Mass.

As Julieta continued her search, she saw something flash near a tree at the end of the block. She blinked hard and wondered if the sun had hit the chrome of a bicycle or baby stroller. Julieta knew from her Monday-through-Saturday power walks that the morning light played tricks on her eyes so that a small dog curled on a porch could look like a large cat, or a stranger might resemble a long-lost friend or relative. And there it was again! A flash, this time brighter than before. Julieta should have been frightened but, instead, she seemed drawn to it, whatever *it* might be. Now the flash became a constant glow hovering at the curb by an empty spot, the only one on the entire street. Julieta glided her Lexus into the opening and parked with the kind of ease she seldom experienced in Los Angeles. It was as if someone had gently taken control of the steering wheel.

Julieta got out and walked to the light, which began to pulsate, first slowly, then faster the closer she got. The light hovered near the base of a large but neatly pruned Guadalupe palm at the edge of a white, wood-framed house. A Realtor's sign stood at attention in the middle of a thick lawn that glistened with dew. With a sudden flash, the light disappeared. Julieta blinked to adjust her eyes. And it was then that she saw her, clear as can be. Where the light had hovered now stood a woman, no more than four feet tall, draped in purple and yellow fabric that looked so soft Julieta wanted to nestle her face into its gentle folds. But she did not. Rather, Julieta approached the woman until she stood not more than two yards from her. The woman slowly lifted her arms, palms up, until she looked like a small "t." And then she moved her lips.

"What?" said Julieta.

The small woman moved her lips again.

"Oh," Julieta answered. "That's what I thought you said."

With that, Julieta turned and walked slowly toward the church. She didn't look back but she could feel the woman staring at her. For a moment, Julieta's mind filled with questions but they quickly slipped away like so much water down a drain.

Julieta got to the church a few minutes after the Mass had started. She found a seat in the back so as to avoid the priest's glare of disapproval. Eventually, her mind drifted to what had happened. The little woman looked so familiar yet like no person Julieta had ever seen before. She wondered if she'd indeed witnessed a miracle, an apparition of La Virgen. But how could this be? Even if Julieta believed in sacred visions—a topic she'd never fully explored— why would the mother of Jesus intervene in her simple life just to find a parking space for the Lexus? Weren't there bigger fish to fry? The war in Iraq? Homelessness? Drug addiction? Bribery in Washington? No. It must have been fatigue or even the onset of a cold or flu.

But what if she'd really seen her? What should Julieta make of those strange words the woman had uttered? Words strung together in a short, precise sentence that could, in all its simplicity, imply a thousand different things depending on one's mood and circumstances of the moment. After Mass, Julieta hurried to her car. There stood the Guadalupe palm, solitary save for two fat pigeons that pecked for breakfast at its base. A Realtor was depositing pink flyers in a plastic tray beneath the FOR SALE sign. She perked up when she noticed Julieta.

"Good morning!" she chirped.

Julieta jumped, turned to the Realtor, and nodded.

"Beautiful morning, isn't it?" the Realtor added as she admired Julieta's Lexus. Julieta reached into her purse, found her keys, and quickly embedded herself into the cocoon safety of her car. As she drove off, Julieta spied the Realtor in the rearview mirror and noticed that she was a rather small woman, almost childlike in stature, not unlike the figure who had appeared in a flash of light. As she drove, Julieta attempted to make sense of it all. Had the mother of Jesus truly revealed herself to this middle-aged wife and mother of twins right here in the heart of Los Angeles? But this apparition didn't resemble the only vision of Mary that Julieta believed in: La Virgen de Guadalupe. Rather than wearing the emerald, gold, and rose garments of La Virgen, this one draped herself in purple and yellow, the color of the Lakers. And instead of looking like a brown-skinned Aztec woman, Julieta's apparition was fair and bore a striking resemblance to Katie Couric. Was she losing her mind? Did dementia suddenly strike Julieta the way it did her great-aunt Josefina who, at her fiftieth-birthday celebration, showed up wearing nothing but a lovely cloth belt and a new pair of patent leather shoes. ¡No! Julieta was not going mad. But there had to be a logical explanation lurking out there for her to discover. The answer would be simple, based on reality, not miracles.

As Julieta and Manuel ate lunch in their kitchen, she struggled to come up with a way to mention her vision without planting suspicions in her husband's head that his wife was totalmente loca. She remembered her mother's advice to approach men as if they were young boys and use small sentences, raise modest ideas. Though Julieta respected Manuel too much to treat him as such, perhaps desperate times required desperate measures.

"Mi cielo," she began, "the sermon was quite good this morning."

"Oh?" said Manuel without looking up from his bowl of posole. Though he tried not to show it, he immediately grew wary. "What did that priest say?"

"He talked about milagros," she fibbed.

Manuel put his spoon down and looked at Julieta. She averted her eyes.

"What about miracles," said Manuel.

"Well," she continued, "he said miracles can happen today just like they did in the Bible."

Manuel scratched his forehead. "¿Y qué más?"

"Not much more than that."

"Sounds like a short sermon," said Manuel as he picked up his spoon and started eating again.

"What do you think?"

"I think he's a fool."

"No, not the priest," Julieta sighed. "The miracle thing. Do you believe that they can happen today?"

"Of course," he said.

Ah! Manuel believed in miraculous events! She had no reason to fear his reaction to her own, personal brush with the holy. But before Julieta could tell him everything about this morning, her husband looked up and added with a laugh: "And I believe in Santa Claus, el cucuy, y el chupacabra."

"Oh," she said.

"Delicious posole," said Manuel with a smile. "Perfecto."

"Thank you," she said. "Glad you like it."

After lunch, Julieta decided to go downtown and do a little shopping. Losing weight had its blessings including the need to buy new clothes for her shrinking figure. As she drove on Pico Boulevard, Julieta passed the church. She thought about the words spoken by that mysterious woman. Julieta shook her head. No more of this silliness. Time to enjoy the sales. And enjoy them she did.

That evening, Julieta came home to a dark house and then remembered that Manuel had plans to see Tomás. She dumped her bulging shopping bags on the bed. Julieta appreciated the quiet after the bustle of shopping downtown. She opened one bag and pulled out a skirt and blouse. Julieta slid out of her clothes and put on the new outfit. Perfect! She posed this way and that and appreciated the results of her exercise regimen. Lights flashed through the bedroom window and then a car pulled into the driveway. Manuel. A bit early. She listened as the front door opened and closed.

"Julieta," called Manuel.

"In here!"

Manuel came to the bedroom doorway and stopped to admire his wife.

"You're home early," said Julieta as she kept her eyes on the mirror.

"Tomás wasn't feeling too well so we called it a night after one beer."

Julieta turned around slowly with her arms held out as if she were about to fly.

"And your sister called before I went out," he added.

"You like?"

"What?"

"My new outfit."

Manuel walked up to Julieta and grabbed her hands.

"Beautiful," he said.

Julieta gave Manuel a broad grin. "Really?"

"Sí, mi amor," said Manuel as he brought Julieta close to him.

"Not bad for a fifty-something-year-old woman?"

"Perfect."

"The truth?" she asked, letting out a little laugh.

"Sí," he said as he pulled her in tighter. "Es la verdad."

Manuel's breath smelled slightly of beer. As Julieta looked at him, her mind fell back to the words spoken by that miraculous little woman who located a perfect parking space for her earlier that day. The woman had said: "This is where you belong."

Julieta caressed Manuel's cheek and he turned slightly to kiss her hand.

"This is where I belong," she said to her husband.

"Me, too," said Manuel. "Me, too."

4

How to Date a Flying Mexican

Rule 1: Don't Tell Anyone about the Flying Part

After the second night Conchita witnessed Moisés flying in his backyard under the moonlight, and after the first night they shared her bed (which happened to be the second night she witnessed him flying in his backyard under the moonlight), she realized that no one, not even her sister Julieta, could learn of her new novio's extraordinary talent. What would people think? Certainly gossip would spread throughout the neighborhood, eventually migrating south out of Los Angeles and down below the border to Conchita's hometown of Ocotlán via whispered phone calls, wisecracking e-mails, and even terse though revealing postcards. Yes, the chisme would most certainly creep out of the city limits, inexorably spreading like a noxious fog, finally reaching all of her friends and family, who would shake their collective head about poor Conchita Lozano de la Peña finally going loca. And, of course they would proclaim, such madness involved lust. See what happens when you don't settle down like all good Catholic Mexican women and marry a man who can give you children and something to look forward to in old age! No God-fearing woman should enter her sixth decade of life—as Conchita had two years earlier—without having walked down the aisle to accept the sacrament of marriage. And it makes no matter that Conchita certainly doesn't look her age with skin as smooth as Indian pottery combined with a voluptuous figure that would knock the false teeth out of any mature (and eligible) man. But that's the problem, you see. Too much fun, not enough pain. And now Conchita thinks she has fallen in love with a Mexican who can fly. ¡Ay Chihuahua!

So, you see, no one can find out about her novio's penchant for flying. Period. Conchita's good fortune cannot be tarnished by this slightly odd behavior. While keeping this secret, she will proudly introduce him to her comadres at tardeadas, quinceañeras, and funerals even if they already recognized Moisés Rojo as Conchita's recently widowed but still vigorous next-door neighbor. And people will, indeed, nod with approval because this woman (¡finalmente!) has found a solid, handsome, and age-appropriate gentleman who maybe—just maybe—will ask her to marry him. And perhaps—they will say—Conchita will come to her senses after all these years of "dating" charming but useless men and allow the Holy Catholic and Apostolic Church to bless their union in a proper Mexican wedding. Because in God's eyes, it is never too late for sinners as long as they are still living and breathing and taking up space on this miraculous place we call Earth.

When Conchita finally broached the subject with Moisés—about his flying, not marriage—he held up his right hand, palm out to his new love, and corrected her: "I do not fly, mi amor," he said softly. "I levitate."

"And what exactly is the difference?" she asked.

"Planes fly," he explained. "Birds and mosquitoes and kites fly. People levitate."

"Oh," said Conchita. "That's clear. But what should I tell people?"

Moisés only shrugged. A few minutes later, when Conchita attempted to return to the topic, Moisés grabbed her shoulders and kissed her full on the mouth. Conchita surrendered to his taste, smell, and touch as if this were their first kiss. Moisés pulled back and looked into his novia's eyes.

"Tell people whatever you wish," he said. "To me, it makes no difference."

And so it was: Conchita decided never to share her secret with anyone.

Rule 2: Don't Try to Understand How He Does It

Other than the flying part, Conchita found Moisés to be quite normal. He ate, slept, read the paper, and loved her as any ordinary man would. When Conchita asked him one day why she couldn't fly unless she held his hand (in which case she would rise effortlessly from the earth as if she were filled with helium), Moisés, of course, corrected her terminology ("I levitate, I don't fly") and then explained that after his wife died, he had fallen out of balance. So he took up yoga and transcendental meditation.

"How did you learn of these things?" asked Conchita.

"I went online to Ask.com and typed in: OUT OF BALANCE," he said. "I found many excellent Web sites and articles."

"And?" Conchita pressed.

"And after much study, I became a disciple."

"A disciple of what?"

"Of balance, mi amor," Moisés answered. "Balance."

"And if I studied yoga and transcendental meditation," ventured Conchita, "I, too, could learn to fly?"

"Of course not," he said. "I read nothing of levitation. It just happened one night as I sat in the lotus position while chanting my mantra."

Conchita skipped asking what a mantra was but nonetheless continued her cross-examination on the crucial issue at hand: "Must you have moonlight to fly?"

"No, no," said Moisés, betraying a bit of impatience. "This is not magic. It is pure physics."

"I knew it!" exclaimed Conchita. "No magic, just magnetic fields, right?"

At this, Moisés simply sniffed and reached for his cup of coffee. Conchita stood at her kitchen sink waiting for an answer to her question.

"You make the richest coffee I've ever tasted," Moisés finally offered. "What do you do to make it so delicious?"

"It's my mother's little secret," she said, pleased by the compliment but annoyed at the evasion.

Sensing Conchita's conflicting emotions, Moisés said: "Magnetic fields could certainly be at work."

To this, Conchita smiled and refilled her lover's cup with fresh coffee.

Rule 3: Don't Lie about It to Your Dead Mother

On the third night they shared her bed, Conchita's late mother, Belén, appeared to her daughter. Moisés snored softly, curled up like a milk-drowsed baby, while Conchita sat by his side, propped up on two pillows, surveying her new and quite delightful situation. And then, in a blink, there stood Belén at the foot of her bed dressed in the pretty floral print she'd been buried in, holding a cup of coffee and puffing on a fat, hand-rolled cigarette.

"Ay, mija," said Belén after she exhaled a large billow of white smoke. "Another man?"

"Mamá," whispered Conchita. "How long have you been watching?"

"Oh, mija, I saw the whole thing."

"¡Ay Dios mío!" exclaimed Conchita through tight lips. "This is so embarrassing!"

"Don't worry, mija," said Belén. "I'm dead. Nothing embarrasses me. You ought to see what your sisters do."

Conchita was partially placated by this thought but she wondered if, in fact, her younger sisters really enjoyed themselves with their men and whether they were having more fun than she. But her mother interrupted such musings.

"So, mija, your new man flies, eh?"

"I don't know what you mean, Mamá," said Conchita as she crossed her arms and turned to gaze upon a slumbering Moisés.

"Don't lie to your mother," said Belén. "The Fourth Commandment forbids it, as it is numbered by the Roman Catholic Church."

Silence.

"It is useless anyway," reasoned Belén. "I know all. Mothers always do." Conchita knew that her mother spoke the truth.

"So, otra vez, mija, I ask you: Does your new man fly?"

"If mothers know all," said Conchita with a sly smile, "why do you ask?"

"Because mothers want their children to admit things," she scolded. "Does your novio fly?"

"No, Mamá, he levitates," said Conchita as she turned to face her mother.

"Planes fly. And so do mosquitoes and birds and other things. But people levitate."

"Ni modo," said Belén with a wave of her cigarette. "It's all the same. He's up in the air like a plane or a bird or a mosquito or whatever." With that, Belén sipped her coffee and let out a little burp.

"But his special talent doesn't make him a bad person, Mamá," said Conchita, feeling a bit defensive.

"You're right," said Belén. "Sabes qué, mija, before I met your papá, I dated a man who could do things with his mouth that were simply miraculous."

"No, Mamá, I don't need to hear this."

"Oh, mija, that man," continued Belén, "that man could make *me* fly!"

Belén let out a little laugh as her mind wandered to ancient memories. And Conchita let out a sigh.

"His name was Francisco," said Belén after a few moments.

Conchita blinked. "You mean the butcher?"

Belén nodded, took another sip of coffee, and then puffed heartily on her fat cigarette. At that moment, Moisés woke with a start.

"Did you say something?" he asked without opening his eyes.

Belén blew a kiss to her daughter and disappeared.

"No, mi cielo," said Conchita. "Back to sleep, it was nothing."

"Have you been smoking?" asked Moisés as he sniffed the air.

"No, mi cielo, no," said Conchita as she pushed down her pillows and snuggled near her man. "You know I don't smoke."

Moisés closed his eyes and started to snore softly.

Rule 4: Don't Grow Weak in Your Resolve to Keep the Secret

Each morning before 7:30 a.m. except on Sundays, Conchita asks Moisés to go back home. It's not because she doesn't appreciate the intimacy that only long, lazy hours in bed can bring. No. It's because her sister Julieta drops by each morning at 7:30 a.m. sharp, Monday through Saturday, to end her power walk and have a little chat with her hermana. After sharing a little family time, Julieta walks home, showers, and meets her husband at their camera shop for another full day of keeping their fussy customers happy. Having Moisés leave before Julieta arrives is not for Julieta's benefit. Not at all. Julieta knows that, throughout the years, her older sister has enjoyed almost countless men. And being sisters, they have shared many naughty stories, though most of them came from Conchita, not Julieta. In reality, Conchita wanted to spare Moisés the embarrassment of having to socialize with Julieta after spending the night in Conchita's warm, entertaining bed. He was a sensitive man who read books, enjoyed art, and, most important, was still healing from his wife's death though he tried mightily to hide his grief from Conchita.

So, Conchita would wake to her buzzing alarm clock at 6:00 a.m., slide herself on top of Moisés for a delicious bit of lovemaking, serve a wonderful breakfast of tamales de puerco and hot coffee along with the newspaper, and then direct her man out the front door. Moisés obliged without argument, subdued by love, food, and the morning news. He'd walk next door to his home, shower, and then meditate in his living room while Conchita and Julieta visited with each other.

During the first two weeks Conchita had enjoyed her new relationship, Julieta used her morning visits to pepper her older sister with questions. Julieta's preliminary queries were somewhat benign and quite general, such as: "Does he snore?" And: "What's his favorite food?" But then after a couple of days, Julieta dug deep with: "How often do you make love?" And: "How big a wedding do you want?" Such questions didn't bother Conchita. Indeed, she'd be insulted if Julieta failed to probe into her love life. But one morning, she surprised Conchita with a particularly insightful query.

"What makes Moisés different from all the other men you've been with?" she asked as Conchita served coffee.

This was precisely the kind of question that Conchita had feared. She'd always shared with Julieta the deepest, most personal elements of her dating life even though Julieta, after drinking up every delicious detail, would eventually scold her older sister for not settling down. Would it hurt if Conchita revealed this little secret to her best audience? What's the worst that could happen? Julieta would think she's crazy? No big deal. But perhaps Conchita shouldn't move too fast on this. Maybe she could drop little crumbs of information to see how Julieta reacts.

"He's very spiritual," answered Conchita, relying on every ounce of self-control that she could muster.

Julieta perked up. "Spiritual?" she asked. "You mean he prays to todos los santos and goes to Mass a lot?"

"Not quite," answered Conchita, looking over to the kitchen window.

"Well, what do you mean, hermana?"

Conchita turned back to her sister, brought the coffee cup to her lips, and said: "He meditates."

"Meditates?"

Conchita drank and then slowly lowered her cup until it met the wooden tabletop with a muffled *clink*. She nodded and waited.

"Meditates?" Julieta spat out again. "What is he, some kind of . . . of . . . of . . . agnostic?"

"Well, I wouldn't say that."

"But, meditation?" continued Julieta. "What kind of man meditates? What's wrong with saying a rosary? That works for me. It works for all good Catholics, right? A good rosary and I'm ready for bed and a good night's sleep."

At that moment, Conchita realized that it would be a mistake to tell her sister that in addition to meditation, Moisés also levitated. So much for sharing.

Rule 5: Don't Google the Word "Levitation"

The same morning Conchita decided, once and for all, that it would be best not to share with Julieta her little secret, she decided to do some research on her novio's special talent. She typed in "levitation" on Google and got over two million hits. Too many to go through. How could she limit her search? Ah! One of the books Moisés loved to read was entitled *The Gateway to Eastern Mysticism*. Conchita added the words "eastern mysticism" to "levitation" and got 5,263 hits. Much more manageable. After going through several Web sites, she found one that seemed promising. The first paragraph explained this phenomenon:

> The reported instances of levitations have been observed in connection with hauntings, shamanistic trances, mystical rapture, mediumship, magic, bewitchments, and (of course) possessions of various types (e.g., satanic or demonic). Based on documented events, many if not most levitations last a short

time, perhaps only a few seconds or minutes. In the field of parapsychology, levitation is considered by many as a phenomenon of telekinesis, also known as "mind over matter."

The first part sent an electrical current of panic through Conchita's entire body. Hauntings? Satanic possessions? ¡Dios mío! What did she get herself into? She pushed on:

Not a small number of saints and mystics reportedly levitated as proof of God's great power over the incarnate form, in holy rapture, or because of their saintly nature. Reputable reports documented the abilities of the seventeenth-century saint Joseph of Cupertino, who could levitate. Indeed, the reports indicated that he could fly in the air for longer periods of time than ever documented with other similar instances of levitation. Conversely, in Eastern mysticism, levitation is an act made possible by mastering concentration as well as breathing techniques that are at the core of the universal life energy.

Ah! Saints! Perhaps Moisés was a modern santo! Conchita wiped her upper lip with the back of her hand and began to calm down. Maybe levitation wasn't so odd after all. She went to Wikipedia, typed in "St. Joseph of Cupertino," and read:

Saint Joseph of Cupertino (Italian: San Giuseppe da Copertino) (June 17, 1603–September 18, 1663) was an Italian saint. He was said to have been remarkably unclever, but prone to miraculous levitation and intense ecstatic visions that left him gaping. In turn, he is recognized as the patron saint of air travelers, aviators, astronauts, people with a mental handicap, test takers, and weak students. He was canonized in the year 1767.

Conchita read about Joseph's father, who was a carpenter and a charitable man. But he died before poor Joseph was even born, leaving his wife, Francesca Panara, "destitute and pregnant with the future saint." Conchita eventually came to this:

As a child, Joseph was remarkably slow witted. He loved God a lot and built an altar. This was where he prayed the rosary. He suffered from painful ulcers during his childhood. After a hermit applied oil from the lamp burning before a picture of Our Lady of Grace, Joseph was completely cured from his painful ulcers. He was given the pejorative nickname "the Gaper," due to his habit of staring blankly into space. He was also said to have had a violent temper.

Such miserable lives these saints lived, thought Conchita. Clearly, that's why they became santos. ¿No? But what of levitation? Conchita wanted to know the details. She scanned the article further, her heart beating fast. This Joseph of Cupertino was a real misfit who had been teased endlessly by his classmates when he had holy visions at the age of eight. Eight! So young to be seeing things. Because of his bad temper and limited education, he had been turned away, at the age of seventeen, by the Friars Minor Conventuals. Eventually, Joseph was admitted as a Capuchin, but was soon removed when his constant fits of ecstasy proved him unsuitable. In his early twenties, he was admitted into a Franciscan friary near Cupertino. The article continued:

> On October 4, 1630, the town of Cupertino held a procession on the feast day of Saint Francis of Assisi. Joseph was assisting in the procession when he suddenly soared into the sky, where he remained hovering over the crowd. When he descended and realized what had happened, he became so embarrassed that he fled to his mother's house and hid. This was the first of many flights, which soon earned him the nickname "The Flying Saint."

And finally, she read that when this saint heard the names of Jesus or Mary, the singing of hymns during the feast of St. Francis, or while praying at Mass, he would go into a trance and soar into the air, "remaining there until a superior commanded him under obedience to revive." His superiors eventually hid him away because his levitations caused great public disturbances. But he also gave off a sweet smell because he was pure. Poor St. Joseph of Cupertino! A prisoner of his own holiness. And would that be her new man's fate if anyone discovered his secret? Would the government or even the Catholic Church want to hide Moisés away so as not to cause public disturbances? No, it was clear to Conchita. Moisés must keep his levitation a secret from all. Period. End of story.

Rule 6: Don't Forget to Breathe

Conchita and Moisés made a compact. If she taught him the secret of her delicious coffee, he'd teach her how to meditate. Moisés quickly mastered Conchita's brewing techniques. However, introducing Conchita to the art of meditation was an entirely different affair. Oh, she easily became skilled at sitting in the lotus position due in large part to her great flexibility, which also made her a delight in bed. But Conchita wrestled mightily with the meditation part of it.

"I'm distracted," she complained as she sat on his living room carpet. "I can't keep my mind from bouncing from thing to thing."

Moisés counseled her: "Mi amor, the most important moment in meditation is when you realize that you are, in fact, distracted."

"¡No es cierto!"

"Yes, it is true," he cooed. "Say to yourself: I am now distracted."

"But I can't empty my mind," she protested.

Moisés said, "Meditation is *not* the absence of thought."

Conchita opened her eyes and turned to her man, who kneeled next to her.

"What the hell is it, then?" she asked.

Moisés gently turned Conchita's head, closed her eyes with his fingertips, and pressed his right palm onto her lower back, his left onto her abdomen.

"Don't forget to breathe," he said.

Conchita obeyed her teacher and inhaled deeply.

"Now exhale," he instructed. "Let your thoughts come and go without clinging to them so that you can focus on the meditation."

Conchita inhaled deeply again. And after a few moments, she exhaled with a soft *woosh*.

This is really stupid, she thought. I'm such a pendeja.

"Tomorrow," said Moisés, "we'll discover your mantra."

"Perfecto," said Conchita. "Perfecto."

"Do you mean it?"

"Yes," said Conchita. "I've always wondered what kind of mantra I would have when I grew old and senile."

Summing Up: Let Us Review

First, never, under any circumstances, let anyone know that your new lover can fly. This will cause great consternation with your family and friends and might lead to the government or Catholic Church locking him up to prevent public disturbances.

Second, don't lie to your dead mother about it. She is dead, after all, so she won't be disturbed by the news. Besides, nothing escapes her so you might as well fess up. The Fourth Commandment (as it is numbered by the Roman Catholic Church) is, indeed, the most important one of all. At least for dead mothers, that is.

Third, do not conduct Internet research on your lover's levitation skills. What you find will only cause great agitation and make you perspire profusely. Sometimes controlled ignorance is the only way to get through life.

Fourth, enjoy your flying Mexican. Life is short and we all need to take delight where we can find it. A corollary to this is that you should learn to accept your lover's special talents even if they're annoying.

And finally, we hope that you remember the most important lesson of all: Do not forget to breathe.

5

THE DREAMER

The dream came to Belén most nights, usually when los grillos sang their song during hot evenings and the open windows allowed this uninvited serenade to disturb her sleep. As Belén's papá often told her, a restless night opens the door to bad dreams. "Mija," Adolfo would coo to his only child, "if you keep sleep from your bed, you will be visited by bad dreams. Don't fight sleep. It is your amigo. Let it take you away. You are only ten. You should have nothing but good dreams." He wondered if his daughter listened to too much radio, that wild music from the United States rattling her young brain, Benny Goodman and those other locos with their "swing" mixing up his daughter. What was wrong with good, strong Mexican music? No other country—not even the United States—had such a diversity of traditional musical styles. Who could beat the wonderful mariachis of Jalisco that fill fiestas with laughter and tears all at once? What of corridos that recount the exploits of great Mexican heroes and villains? But Belén, even though quite young, knew that Benny Goodman and swing music were not responsible for her nightmares. No.

And she knew that when the crickets chirped their rhythmic cry, Belén couldn't avoid *that* dream. It would begin in the same way, innocently at first, a bit confusing, and then spin and spiral into something horrible, evil, wicked. The first time she told her parents about it, they both shook their heads in fear and wonder. Belén's mother made a sign of the cross, in fact. But after a few more tellings, they grew a bit bored by the details. Their only concern was that Belén sleep through the night so that she could be awake the next day and not wander about with droopy eyelids, long yawns replacing words.

Belén knew that the only way to cure herself of the nightmare was to find out what it meant. But she had no conception of how to do this. Her parents were of little help. They offered no explanation for what their daughter dreamt.

Belén's best friend, Hortencia, believed that the dream would remain a mystery unless . . . unless . . . she went to Katrina for help.

"The curandera?" said Belén, knowing full well that their town had only one Katrina and she was a curandera of the highest order.

"You have no choice," said Hortencia, nodding in such a way that made her look very wise.

"But," whispered Belén, "they say she's loca."

"The best ones are," Hortencia mused.

"And besides," continued Belén, "all curanderas want payment."

Hortencia thought about this. "Maybe she'd ask for very little because you're little."

Though Belén's fear was great, she did want to know what her dream meant. She pondered the issue of money for a few moments. Finally: "I'll be right back."

She went into the house and saw her mother at the sink, soaking raw pinto beans.

"Mija," said Mónica without looking up, "did Hortencia leave already?"

"No, Mamá," said Belén as she continued toward her bedroom. "She wants to see my doll."

This was a good lie because, in reality, Hortencia hadn't seen it yet. Belén retrieved a tattered sock from beneath her cot and stuck it under her doll's dress. She walked past her mother and out of the house successfully. After she and Hortencia settled safely under the large pine tree that stood a hundred yards from the house, Belén opened the sock and dropped three coins onto the grass.

"¡Ay!" said Hortencia. "Where did you get these?"

"One is from my tío Normando," said Belén as she touched one coin. "And these other two are from my parents, one from my last birthday, and one from the year before."

"You're rich!"

"Would this be enough for Katrina?"

"Oh, yes."

Belén gathered up the coins and dropped them, one by one, into the sock. "Will you come with me?" she said softly as she stuffed the sock under her doll's dress.

Hortencia's eyes widened. She pursed her lips and didn't answer.

"Please?"

"But they say she isn't Mexican."

"What is she?"

Hortencia leaned close: "She's from Russia!"

Belén thought about this. Her parents had mentioned this country of Russia but she couldn't remember why. Many things were happening across the ocean, countries doing bad things, threatening other countries. Belén believed that Mexico was safe from such ugly things. But Katrina couldn't be so Russian to be of any danger. She'd been living near their town for as long as Belén could remember. She must be very Mexican by now, thought Belén.

"Come with me, Hortencia!" pleaded Belén. "Tomorrow is Saturday. We can go anytime."

Hortencia looked toward Belén's house and took a deep breath.

"Sí," she finally said. "Sí."

The next day, the girls walked to a creek-side encampment just outside of town in search of Katrina. As they made their way, Belén and Hortencia exchanged every story they could remember about the curandera. The most notorious tale involved the great tragedy of Lázaro Mayo Cisneros, the famous architect and former mayor whose life was ruined by his maid's jealousy—ruined with the help of Katrina's dark power.

"She had gone to Katrina for magic to remove her master's young wife from the house," whispered Hortencia. "The result was horrible!"

Belén had heard this story.

"And they say that Katrina worships La Santísima Muerte," added Hortencia, "just like the Aztecs did."

"¡No!"

"It's true," said Hortencia. "La Santísima Muerte is a skeleton who wears a white dress."

Belén shuddered. She knew this and other frightening things about Katrina's powers and idolatry. But the curandera also had helped people, this she knew too. There was poor little José who used to suffer from horrible convulsions. But Katrina chanted over him and made the boy chew on dark leaves every day for a month. No more convulsions. Amazing! And certainly Katrina would wish no harm upon a girl such as herself.

As Belén and Hortencia approached the encampment, they noticed several crudely constructed, dilapidated shacks along the creek's banks. As they came closer, they noticed a stench of human filth, which made them gag and caused their eyes to water. Belén hugged her doll closer as Hortencia tightened her grip around Belén's waist. As they entered the encampment itself, ragged men, women, and children wandered about silently, aimlessly, without joy. No one looked up at these two young intruders. Belén finally asked a boy where she could find Katrina. He pointed listlessly to a shack and then continued on his way to who knew where. The girls trudged through the muck to the shack. They finally reached the hovel.

"What do we do now?" said Hortencia, staring at the rotting door.

Before Belén could answer, they heard a grunt from within the shack. The girls jumped back a step.

"Did you hear that?" said Belén.

"It sounded like a person, I think."

The sound came again, but this time the girls realized that it was, indeed, a woman's voice that said simply: "Come in."

The girls looked at each other.

"Come in," said the voice again. "I am here."

Belén pushed the door open, slowly, until it stopped. Boards covered all three windows in a haphazard fashion to thwart sunlight and the curious. The girls let their eyes adjust to the dark until, after a few moments, they discerned a woman sitting at a small table at the far corner of the one-room shack. She was small-framed and fragile-looking and of an unknowable age. Her long hair hung neatly away from her face and down her back. The woman's sharp, green eyes flickered as she lit a lone candle.

"Please," said Katrina. "Come forward and sit here." She motioned toward a bench that stood at the opposite end of the table.

So, this is the great curandera, thought Belén. I've wasted my time for certain!

Katrina let out a low chuckle. "No," she said. "That is what Lázaro's maid thought so long ago but I proved her wrong. And as I told her, you have not wasted your time, I assure you."

The girls' eyes widened and they both took a step back. Katrina chuckled again.

"Please," said Katrina. "Sit. It is time to talk of what you need."

The girls had no choice. They slowly made their way to the bench and sat as directed. Katrina smiled, leaned forward, and said softly, almost gently, to Belén: "You have come to me to understand the meaning of your dream."

As these words left Katrina's lips, Belén knew that this great curandera would help her. Belén nodded. The curandera suddenly clapped twice, loudly, making the girls jump.

"Payment first," said Katrina, pointing to the doll.

Belén pulled the sock from beneath her doll's dress and dropped the three coins onto the table. They rolled around, noisily, until all three lay flat on the gnarled wood. The curandera let out a small laugh and slowly gathered up the coins into her left hand. She examined the coins, bobbed her hand up and down as if to weigh them, and then closed her hand into a tight little fist.

"Now tell me," said Katrina as she leaned back and closed her eyes. "Tell me your dream."

Belén turned to Hortencia for encouragement but her friend sat frozen, eyes glued to the curandera. Belén turned back to Katrina. Belén's tongue stuck to the back of her mouth; she tried unsuccessfully to separate her lips. Katrina sat quietly, waiting. Finally, Belén cleared her throat, wet her lips, and started: "In my dream, I watch my tío Normando dance, head back, eyes closed, arms out as if holding a woman, though he holds no one. But this does not seem to bother him. He dances, a step forward, a step to the left, spinning slowly to a song only he can hear."

Katrina nodded and let out a little grunt. "Where does he dance?"

"In a beautiful, green field, the one near my house."

"Continue."

"And then I hear a horse galloping but I see nothing. It gets louder and louder until finally it sounds as if a horse is right before me but I still see nothing. Tío Normando stops dancing and opens his eyes. He searches for the horse, too, I am sure, because now the loud galloping is almost unbearable. And then, in a flash, there it is: a magnificent white stallion off on the horizon, mounted with a beautiful saddle but no rider. Tío Normando sees the stallion and lets out a shriek, a bellow, a sound I do not recognize as his voice because it is so horrible. I wonder why the stallion frightens him. It is a beautiful beast, so powerful, galloping with great strength and purpose off on the horizon."

"Is there more?" said Katrina, keeping her eyes shut.

"Yes."

"What?"

Belén hesitated. Hortencia turned to her friend as if to urge her on. Finally, Belén concluded: "The stallion disappears, just like that, with a galloping sound that grows fainter by the moment. And my tío calms, his bellowing going silent, until I hear neither the stallion nor my tío. And then he does it."

"What?" said Katrina. "What does he do?"

"He closes his eyes, raises his arms to embrace an invisible partner, and starts to dance again just as before the stallion appeared."

"There's more?" the curandera said.

Belén hesitated, and then: "I feel a heavy hand on my shoulder so I turn and look up. It's my papá. He looks down at me."

"What does he say?"

"Nothing," said Belén. "He just shakes his head and looks sad. And then I wake."

Katrina's eyes popped open. Then she did something that surprised the girls: She smiled.

"Do you know what it means?" Belén said to the curandera.

"Yes."

Belén leaned close to Katrina, no longer afraid. "What?"

Katrina rubbed her chin and seemed to plan her answer carefully. "You have the gift too," she finally said.

Belén shook her head. "I have no gifts."

"You know what the dream means," said Katrina. "But its meaning frightens you, as it should, so you do not trust your own knowledge."

"What?"

"Here," Katrina said, opening her fist to reveal the three coins. "Take these back. You do not need my help."

"But I do!"

Katrina dropped the coins onto the table.

Belén grew frantic: "Tell me what it means!"

Katrina stood and walked to a small bed. She hesitated, as if pondering her next move, and then sat, easing herself down slowly onto the creaky bed. Katrina let out a sigh.

"You must leave now," she said.

Hortencia stood and tried to lift Belén to her feet. Belén refused to move.

"Leave now!" yelled Katrina.

Belén leapt up, stumbled, and reached for the table to balance herself. She quickly gathered up the coins but couldn't move her feet. Hortencia pulled at her friend and before they realized it, the girls stood outside the shack. A small crowd had formed outside Katrina's shack, finally curious.

"We have to leave," said Hortencia. "Now!"

Belén didn't argue. She clutched the doll and ran with her friend away from Katrina's shack. They didn't stop running until they reached Belén's home. The girls threw themselves under the pine tree, giddy with fright. In silence, they both allowed images of Katrina to wander through their minds.

"Well," Hortencia finally said, "do you?"

"Do I what?"

"Do you know what your dream means?"

Belén shook her head. Hortencia sat up.

"You must!" she said. "The curandera knew too much to be wrong about that!"

Belén hugged the doll and she searched her mind. No, she didn't know what the dream meant. Katrina made a mistake. Nothing more. Hortencia stood and wiped grass and dirt from her dress. She stared at Belén in the same way she had stared at Katrina: in fear and wonder.

"What?" said Belén.

"The curandera said you had the gift."

Belén stood and moved closer to her friend.

"You're just like Katrina," said Hortencia as she took a step back.

"No," Belén said.

Hortencia turned and started toward the dirt road. "I have to go home," she said without looking back.

"Wait," said Belén.

"No," answered Hortencia. "Mamá will be angry. I need to go."

She was soon out of sight. Belén sighed and walked to the house. Her mother was nowhere to be found. Probably at the mercado shopping for dinner. Belén's father had to work for half a day this Saturday but had two more hours at the Velasco ranch before coming home. She entered her bedroom and placed the doll carefully onto the cot. Belén pulled the sock from beneath the doll's skirt and hid her little treasure again. At least Katrina had returned the money. That means she must be good, figured Belén. Strange and frightening, but good.

Belén took off her muddy shoes and got on top of the cot. Her papá promised that when she was older, he would make a real bed for her from strong pinewood. He'd even travel to the Federal District to buy a mattress for it. And Belén knew that her papá could do it because he could do anything. She fantasized about such a magnificent bed, one that Hortencia would be jealous of. But right then, her cot felt perfect. Belén thought of her favorite uncle and wondered why he kept appearing in her dreams. Why did the stallion frighten him so? And why did he dance with an invisible partner? What did it all mean? If she had a gift, it wasn't working. Maybe in time, Belén would know how to use her powers, if she had powers.

As these thoughts bounced through her mind, she grew drowsy. She envisioned handsome tío Normando, not the frightened man of her dreams, but the brave younger brother of her papá, strong and sure of himself. A man who was afraid of no one, and certainly not frightened of a stallion without a rider. He would live a long, important life, filled with great deeds and many friends. Maybe once Belén became a woman, her tío would fall in love with her and take Belén as his beautiful bride. Hortencia had ridiculed this plan many times before, saying that uncles did not marry their nieces because it was a sin. In fact,

Hortencia had opined, Belén could go to hell just by thinking about it. But what did she know? Everything frightened Hortencia. Belén pulled her doll close, kissed its cheek, and sighed deeply. Within a few moments, she snored softly and drifted into a perfect, dreamless sleep.

That night, after dinner, Belén went to bed believing that she was cured of her nightmare. Her parents tucked Belén into bed, said a prayer, and kissed their only child. Before leaving Belén's bedroom, Adolfo opened the window to relieve his daughter of the night's heat. The crickets' song spilled in and washed over the girl, but she no longer feared the noisy insects. Her sleep would be filled only with good dreams, she knew this for certain.

But the dream came back. There was her tío Normando dancing in an open field with a phantom partner moving to the rhythm of phantom music. And she could hear the galloping stallion coming closer until finally it appeared off on the horizon. As Belén waited for her uncle to begin his horrid bellowing, suddenly all went quiet. The stallion stood still, not moving a hair. Her uncle stopped dancing, dropped his hands, and waited, silently. He then turned to Belén, pointed to a spot past his niece's left shoulder, and nodded. Belén turned and saw her father standing a few yards away. She studied his face and noticed that tears flowed down his cheeks. Her father wept without a sound, eyes shifting from his younger brother and then to his daughter and then back again.

And at that moment, Belén understood the meaning of her dream. It all made sense, as much sense as anything she knew about life. The dream's meaning filled her with a heaviness, a weight she fought, but to no avail. Yes, Belén understood her dream and she vowed to forget its importance. Because if she did not, she would not be able to continue living. And Belén would keep this vow until life's events prevented her from doing so any longer.

6

Los Dos

Julieta pulled her sons together in a tight hug. Rolando and Mateo groaned but reciprocated by squeezing their mother, sighing in unison and then ultimately accepting her love. When they were little, the twins couldn't wait to be embraced by their mother. But as freshmen in college standing in the middle of Westwood midday on a bright, sunny Tuesday just outside UCLA's sprawling campus for all the world to see, such public demonstrations of maternal affection embarrassed them in a way only similarly situated teenagers could understand. But they were powerless. They had no choice in the matter. Julieta loosened her grip, leaned back, and looked up toward her sons, first Rolando and then Mateo. Identical in almost every way.

"Ay, so big," she said.

The twins looked down at their mother.

"Los Dos," she added.

"Got class, Mom," said Mateo.

Julieta sighed.

"Me, too," said Rolando.

Mateo rubbed Julieta's left shoulder. "Say hi to Pop."

"Yep," said Rolando. "Say hi to Pop."

Julieta nodded, turned, and *click-clicked* toward the parking lot.

Mateo looked at his brother's face. "You've got lipstick on your cheek," he said.

"You, too," said Rolando.

Mateo's cell phone let out two beeps. He pulled the phone out of his shirt pocket, flipped it open, and smiled.

"Who's texting?" asked Rolando as he tried to look at the little screen but the bright sunlight kept him from deciphering anything. "Lisa?"

"No," said Mateo as he punched in a quick response. "Lucy. She wants me to get to her room ASAP."

"What happened to Lisa?"

Mateo snapped his phone closed. "Nothing."

Rolando shook his head. "Does Lisa know about Lucy?"

"Do I look like a pendejo to you?"

"I take that as a 'no.' "

Rolando started to walk toward campus. Mateo followed.

"We have Econ," said Rolando. "In fifteen minutes."

"And I've got Lucy right now," smiled Mateo. "Her roommate is gone for two hours so I have to take advantage of this."

"Lucy and Lisa and whoever are going to make you flunk out and then what?"

"Baby bro," said Mateo as he patted Rolando's shoulder, "when you get a girlfriend, you'll understand."

"I'm three minutes younger than you," said Rolando without smiling. "And you're apparently dating for the both of us."

"Ain't nothing stopping you from getting hooked up with a hot frosh," laughed Mateo. "You're muy guapo, chico."

"And what does that make you?"

"Muy guapo, también. Except I'm a better dresser."

Rolando just shook his head.

"Do me a favor," said Mateo as he started to diverge from his brother's path.

"What now?"

"Take good notes."

"And do me a favor."

Mateo stopped in his tracks. "Anything, baby bro. Name it."

"Choose one girl and stick with her."

Mateo chuckled, winked, and broke into a trot. "Whatever," he said over his shoulder.

Rolando watched Mateo head down the street. "Whatever," he said to himself. "Whatever."

◧

As Rolando listened to the lecture and took notes, he regretted signing up for any class that Mateo took. They had Econ and Chicana/Chicano Studies 10A together, which were two courses too many. When they attended Loyola High School, Mateo took advantage of Rolando's inability to utilize a bit of tough love with his twin. Rolando couldn't let Mateo sink or swim. Mateo's problem was that he enjoyed life too much. But he was also a quick study and could pull an A in most classes by studying Rolando's notes. Rolando was the pendejo. No question. Maybe he should enjoy himself a little, too. But that would disturb the balance of the universe, the yin-yang of their twinhood. No. Things were going to remain the same as long as "Los Dos" roamed this earth.

"Did I miss much?"

Rolando turned to his right as a student settled in next to him.

"Not too much."

"This guy is so boring, it's hard to make myself get here on time."

Rolando nodded and turned back to the PowerPoint screen. The professor prowled the stage using a remote to operate the laptop. Rolando wondered how many students sat in the auditorium. A hundred? Two hundred?

"I'm Josh, by the way."

Rolando looked down and saw a large, pale hand extended over his notes. He turned and looked at Josh, who offered a wide, toothy grin. Rolando took the hand and shook it.

"Rolando," he said.

"Cool," said Josh as he squeezed Rolando's hand. "This school is so huge, I don't really feel like I know anyone. Back home, we were always in everybody's business."

"Where's home?"

"Fresno."

"You're not in Kansas anymore," said Rolando as he released Josh's hand.

"Clearly not," said Josh.

Rolando turned back to face the front of the class. After a minute, Josh did the same.

▣

"Who is this?" asked Mateo.

Lucy reached over Mateo's chest and snatched the CD case from the nightstand. She held it over Mateo's face so he could see the cover. As she did this, the blanket slowly slid off Lucy's shoulder and Mateo quickly turned away from the CD case to enjoy the view. Lucy pulled the blanket back over her breasts.

"Look here," she said, shaking the CD case for emphasis. "Lila Downs. Her new album."

Mateo turned and examined the case.

"You like?"

"Yeah," said Mateo, sounding a little surprised at his answer.

"Lila Downs is the Frida Kahlo of music."

"No doubt."

Lucy put the case back on the nightstand and slid down and snuggled into Mateo.

"We've got thirty minutes before Krystal gets back," she said.

"Where's your third roommate?"

Lucy scratched her nose. "Haven't seen her in two weeks."

"Worried?"

"Nope. Krystal found out from someone who knows Doreen that she's going to drop out anyway. Hates college."

"Oh."

"Just a matter of time before they send someone to get her stuff."

"Oh."

Lucy extricated herself from Mateo's arms and got up on one elbow to look down at him.

"Te amo," she said.

Mateo blinked hard.

"Te amo," Lucy said again.

Mateo smiled and touched Lucy's cheek.

"You're special to me, Lisa," he said.

Lucy's eyes bulged. "What?" she sputtered.

"Huh?"

Lucy scampered out of the bed and grabbed her bathrobe.

"Get out!"

"What's wrong?" said Mateo as he sat up.

Lucy pulled her robe tightly around her tiny body.

"My name is *Lucy*," she said. "Not *Lisa*."

"Crap," muttered Mateo.

He tried to say something else but Lucy held up her right hand.

"Don't even," she said. "Don't even try."

□

Rolando and Josh sat silently at the Kerckhoff Coffee House as they listened to a song playing over the small, overhead speakers. Josh kept his hands wrapped around his cup as he watched the steam rise slowly from the hot coffee. Rolando sipped from his cup. Students and a few faculty members filled every table. Shorts, T-shirts, and flip-flops were the order of the day.

"I don't remember who did it," Josh finally said. "I mean, it's my dad's music. But I know it's that song from that *CSI* show, right?"

Rolando laughed. "It's so easy. Think hard."

"I know the name of the song, I guess."

"Then you have the name of the band that did it."

Josh's face suddenly lit up. Rolando thought that Josh had the most perfect smile he'd ever seen. Where did he get such faultless teeth? Josh had the kind of face that no one could dislike. Open, honest, with clear skin, a few freckles, curly red hair, green eyes. Suddenly, Josh's eyes flickered and his expression quickly morphed into one of shock and then puzzlement. Rolando turned toward the entrance to see what had made Josh react so. And in a second, it made sense: There stood Mateo searching the room frantically. When his eyes met Rolando's, Mateo quickly made it through the crowd to their table.

"Bro, I'm in deep caca," said Mateo as he pulled up a chair.

"My rude twin," said Rolando. "Mateo, this is Josh. He's in our Econ class. But you wouldn't know that."

"You two are identical," said Josh as he nodded in Mateo's direction.

Mateo returned Josh's nod and continued: "We got to talk. I messed up with Lisa, I mean, Lucy. It's pretty bad, bro."

Rolando turned to Josh, who seemed to be at a loss.

"My twin is dating two women at the same time and he has apparently been found out."

Mateo looked down at his hands.

"And only a few hours ago I warned him about his ways," said Rolando, enjoying his brother's anguish.

Mateo looked at Josh. "Give me your opinion, free from brotherly bias and preaching."

"Shoot," said Josh.

"Have you ever been in total lust with two girls at the same time?" began Mateo.

Rolando studied Josh's face and wondered what he would say.

Josh shook his head. "I can honestly answer that question in the negative."

Mateo sighed. "I guess you're no help."

Josh took a sip of coffee. "But I've been in *love* with two people at the same time. Not the same thing as lust."

Mateo slapped his hand on the table. "Love, lust, whatever. But you know what I mean, right?"

"I guess."

"So," said Mateo, "hypothetically speaking, is it right to make a man choose between two hot, beautiful, sexy girls? I mean, is it?"

Rolando began, "I think . . . "

Mateo held up his hand. "I'm asking Josh, here, bro. Let him answer."

"Well," said Josh, "it all depends."

"On what?" said Mateo as he leaned close for his answer.

"What do the girls want from this hypothetical guy?"

Mateo fell back in his seat. "That's the kind of answer Rolando would give. In other words, no help to me."

Josh looked at his cell phone. "It's late and I got class. Got to run."

"See you Thursday," said Rolando.

"Yep."

After Josh had left, Mateo poked Rolando in the arm.

"Why are you having coffee with a *joto*?"

Rolando felt his face grow hot. "What?"

"Josh. Nice guy and all. But total fag."

Rolando shifted in his seat.

"Look, bro," confided Mateo, "I like all people. I don't care if Josh likes to get a little *Brokeback Mountain* action. Just don't get a reputation."

Rolando stood quickly. "I have to go."

"Hey, don't get mad at me. Just trying to give a little brotherly advice. Something you obviously can't give me."

Rolando swung his backpack over his shoulder. Mateo's cell phone beeped and he pulled it out.

"Who is it now?"

Mateo smiled. "Lisa."

"See ya."

Mateo started to text a response to Lisa. Rolando sighed and walked away. Just before leaving the coffee house, he turned for one more look at his twin who was happily texting Lisa, completely oblivious to the din of the other laughing, chatting patrons. At that moment, Rolando allowed himself to wonder how they could be brothers, let alone identical twins. But he also envied Mateo's ability to switch in a matter of seconds from emotional distress to flirty giddiness. Must be nice.

⊡

FARMBOY: hey, what up?
ROLANDO88: who is this?
FARMBOY: it's me, josh, from econ
ROLANDO88: how u get my email?
FARMBOY: e-z
ROLANDO88: mysterious
FARMBOY: that's me. want to go for a drive?

Rolando looked out of his dorm window. It was a perfect, clear night and he'd finished all the studying that he needed to do. His roommate snored loudly with *Light in August* spread upon his chest, the paperback rising and falling with each heavy breath. Rolando turned back to the laptop.

ROLANDO88: sure . . . why not?
FARMBOY: if you got a car
ROLANDO88: battered green corolla with about 100k on it
FARMBOY: perfect . . . where do u want 2 meet?
ROLANDO88: top of janss steps
FARMBOY: sure
ROLANDO88: kul. ½ hour. k?
FARMBOY: yep ;-)

◧

"I love Wilshire," said Josh as the wind blew his hair back.

Rolando kept his window closed.

"I mean, it changes so much from West L.A. as we move east."

"In a bad way?"

Josh laughed. "No, not in a bad way."

They stopped at a red light. Rolando turned to Josh. Josh leaned back and grinned, enjoying being watched.

"Look at that beautiful Lexus," said Josh.

Rolando turned to the car in front of him.

"My mom has one like that."

"Must be nice."

Rolando leaned forward and squinted.

"Crap," he said.

"What?"

"That *is* my mom's car."

Josh sat up straight and squinted too. "And that's your dad?"

The light turned green. Rolando followed the Lexus but kept back just a bit.

"You're tailing your own parents?" laughed Josh.

"That's not my pop," said Rolando.

"Well, whoever it is, he sure is sitting close to your mom."

Rolando's stomach tightened. He searched his mind for his parents' friends and customers. Who could this man be? And then it happened. Julieta looked into her rearview mirror and saw her son staring back at her. Rolando could see her almost jump out of her seat. Then she reached over to the man and pushed him—she actually pushed him! The man moved away from Julieta and pulled down his visor to look into the mirror. Rolando realized at that moment that a film of perspiration covered his face and forearms.

"Let's turn at Fairfax," whispered Rolando.

"Sure."

"And then we'll take Pico."

"Where to?"

"The beach."

◩

They sat watching the carousel go round. Josh reached into the Bubba Gump bag and pulled out a large onion ring.

"Life is like a bag of onion rings," he said.

Rolando kept his eyes on the carousel. Josh sighed and then bit into the onion ring.

"Want to talk?"

"We used to come here," said Rolando. "I always chose a horse that went up and down."

"And Mateo?"

Rolando smiled a little. "He got sick easily so he always got on one that didn't move, near the edge. And he always made Mom stand right next to him with a hand on his back."

Josh lifted the bag to Rolando. This time, he didn't resist. He reached in and pulled out a small onion ring. He popped it into his mouth and chewed.

"Good?"

Rolando nodded.

"Are you okay?"

The carousel slowly came to a stop. The children waiting in line jumped and squirmed in anticipation of their ride.

"Why did you leave Fresno?" asked Rolando.

"You have to ask?"

Rolando turned to Josh. There it was again. That perfect smile. Those green eyes. Rolando reached over the Bubba Gump bag and softly squeezed Josh's shoulder.

"I'm okay," said Rolando.

Rolando brought back his hand and pulled out another onion ring. This time, he pulled out a large one that would not go down in one gulp. The carousel now had a new group of children safely strapped in with a few adults standing next to several nervous tots. As it picked up speed, Rolando kept his eyes on a little girl who rode a black stallion near the center of the carousel. She gripped with both hands the metal pole that ran through her horse. As it rose and fell, she giggled and blinked. After a few moments, her face grew serious. She frowned just a bit, stuck out her chin, and removed one hand and then the other from the pole. The little girl slowly lifted her arms over her head, relaxed her face, and let out a loud squeal. A man and woman who stood near the carousel offered the girl a cheer, clearly proud of their daughter. And at that moment, as the carousel went round and round, Rolando believed that this little girl, with her arms raised in triumph, her proud parents rooting her on, was simply the bravest person he had ever seen in his entire life.

7

El Cucuy

I'm not certain how it came to this. This thing I can't name. But if you're old enough to marry and have children—that's really the key to understanding what I'm talking about—then you probably could imagine what it means to sit in a room, with no answers, all alone because even your own mother had to get some sleep, certain that you've lost it all—everything that ever mattered—and you feel like vomiting, losing it all right then, but you can't even bring yourself to do that. And the phone doesn't ring, and your husband who is trying to get a plane back from San Francisco hasn't called in almost six hours, and you miss the smell of your daughter's hair mixed with the sweet sweat of a full day running around with the other first-graders, and you try with all your might to remember which blouse you chose for her yesterday morning. Because that's what the police asked you and you felt foolish, like a bad mother, because you couldn't remember. Was it the pink one with Winnie the Pooh on the front pocket or the simple, yellow blouse your mother got for Sofia's last birthday? The shoes you can remember. Black Mary Janes. That's easy. Sofia refused to wear anything else to school. Refuses, I mean. She's like that. Stubborn. Like me.

I remember seeing a TV interview a few years ago of a woman who was so certain her son would be kidnapped by her ex-husband that each morning she chose her son's clothes for the day and took a Polaroid of them laid out on her living room carpet. That way, if the ex did take her son, she could show the picture to the police and say, "See, this is what he was wearing when he got on the school bus this morning." Smart woman. Because it eventually did happen, and the photo helped the police find her son. A gas station attendant just happened to hear the description on the radio and about an hour later noticed that a kid who needed to use the bathroom wore that exact, same outfit. The boy's father waited by his car as he filled it up. The attendant gave the key to the little boy and then called the police. Amazing. But I never could have imagined this happening to me. Why should I? Rigoberto and I are still married, at least for now, so I don't have to worry about an ex trying to take her. So, you see, I don't have a Polaroid or a digital picture and I couldn't remember what she wore. As the officer on the phone waited, I closed my eyes tight trying to conjure up what she looked like when I dropped her off at school. But it was no use. I had to tell the officer that I'd call back after I went through Sofia's closet to figure it out. All I had was a failed memory with too much to worry about each rushed morning to remember what blouse I handed to Sofia. I ran up to her room and ransacked the closet. I didn't do it in the smartest way so I know it took longer than it should have. But I finally figured it out: the yellow blouse and pleated, blue skirt. I called the officer back and told her. She thanked me, told me to stay calm and that a detective would be coming by.

It's too quiet. I won't go back up to her room. I can't. I have to wait by the phone. They're going to let me know if Sofia qualifies for the Amber Alert. They think so, but I don't know if that's a good thing. They finally did send a nice detective over to talk to me. James Rodríguez. He has a slight accent that reminds me of my cousin, Salvador. I wonder if someone doing the paperwork assumed I spoke Spanish better than English based on my last name. So maybe that's why they assigned him to the case. But my Spanish is lousy. I don't know. It doesn't matter. All I know is that nothing can take me away from my vigil. Everything else seems so stupid. Jay Leno. Mr. Santos who lives next door and tries to flirt with me whenever he can. Full-page ads for Dockers and Verizon Wireless and who-knows-what in the *Times*. President Bush saying something about how we're really winning the war but it will take sacrifices. None of it really matters anymore, does it? Can it?

▣

Sofia watches as the man pours a can of SpaghettiOs into the hot frying pan making the oil sizzle and pop. He tosses the empty can in the sink and reaches for one of two eggs that sit on the counter. He taps it gently with the edge of a spoon until a fine crack appears. He sets the spoon down, uses his fingernails to pry open the egg, and allows its contents to splat on the mound of pasta. The man snatches the second egg and repeats the action. He turns to Sofia with a wide smile.

"My own special concoction," says the man in a singsong voice as he stirs the eggs into the SpaghettiOs. "The eggs give it extra protein, which is important for little girls."

Sofia blinks once and then twice. The man turns back to his cooking. He wears a crisp, blue Oxford shirt tucked into Levis, a wide leather belt, but no shoes or socks. Sofia pulls the blanket around her shoulders and shivers. She wishes she had her clothes. Where did he put them? She was too scared to watch what he did with them after he undressed her and put her in bed next to him. And then after he was done he gave her a Kit Kat bar as a reward. But where were her clothes?

"Here it is, sweetie," says the man as he puts a steaming bowl in front of Sofia. "Eat up. It's good for you."

Sofia tightens her lips. Her arms and legs hurt. The man gently places a children's spoon by Sofia's right hand. She looks down at it. It's red plastic with a smiling clown's face on the handle.

"Eat up," repeats the man. "I made it especially for you."

Sofia looks up at him. He has gentle eyes, a round face, neatly trimmed beard and mustache. But his head looks funny. The hair on top is very black and thick but the hair above and around his ears is thin and graying.

"Eat up," he says.

Sofia blinks.

"Eat up, now."

▣

Rigoberto sits at San Francisco International Airport waiting for his flight. The best he could do was eleven o'clock into Burbank. His car is parked at LAX so he'll have to get a taxi. He crosses his arms and looks out at the planes taking off and landing.

"I'm so sorry, baby," says Adelina.

Rigoberto doesn't answer. Adelina tries to snuggle close but he shifts away slightly without uncrossing his arms. Adelina stands.

"I need a Sprite," she says. "Want anything, baby?"

Rigoberto shakes his head and wishes she wouldn't call him "baby." Adelina turns and walks away. Rigoberto shifts his eyes ever so slightly so that he can watch her ass sway left and then right. He notices that other men do the same but without any attempt to hide what they're looking at. One man leans into another and whispers something. They both break out in a low, nasty snicker. Rigoberto can't believe that he's able to think of Adelina in that way while his daughter is missing. And he can't believe that Adelina offered not only to drive him to the airport but to wait with him. That's why he hasn't called Bernadette in so long: He can't get a moment away from Adelina. He's kept his cell phone off the whole time. But now here's his chance. Rigoberto pulls out his cell and turns it on. Three messages. He doesn't need to check them. He calls home. Bernadette picks up on the first ring.

"Hello?"

Rigoberto leans into the phone. "It's me, sweetie. Anything?"

"Where have you been?"

"Trying to get a flight."

Silence. And then: "Still nothing from the police."

Rigoberto grabs his stomach as it gurgles loudly. When did he eat last?

"I have an eleven o'clock into Burbank," he says. "I'll grab a taxi from there."

"Why?" asks Bernadette. But then she remembers that Rigoberto flew out of LAX. "Never mind."

"Yeah."

"I need you here," she whispers.

"Yeah, sweetie, I know," he says, trying to sound comforting. "Bad time to go on business."

"You couldn't have predicted this."

Rigoberto sees Adelina coming back with a can of Sprite and a bag of Doritos.

"I'll call when I land," he says quickly.

"Don't get off the phone," says his wife.

Adelina catches Rigoberto's eye and slows down a few yards away.

"It's too noisy in here," says Rigoberto. "I'll call."

He snaps the phone closed, and then opens it to make certain that it's turned off before putting it in his jacket pocket. Adelina sits down.

"Dorito?" she says as she holds the bag up.

Rigoberto shakes his head and folds his arms tightly across his chest. Adelina shrugs and looks away.

◘

It's times like this that I feel as though I don't know Rigoberto. Why couldn't he stay on the phone with me? I could hear him fine. I look out the window. Across the street I see Conchita walking her adorable whippet past her neighbor's apartment. Who lives there? Oh, yes. That nice widower. Mr. Rojo, that's his last name. What's his first? His late wife was so nice. But near the end, the cancer kept her inside their apartment. All I saw was Mr. Rojo come and go with groceries and whatever else his wife needed. Carmela. That was her name. And . . . Moisés! Moisés Rojo. I wonder if Carmela realized how lucky she was to have that man as her husband. And maybe he'll make a second woman happy. Probably Conchita. Boy, look at her. She really can pull it off. I wouldn't be caught dead in a dress that tight with all those colors. But I don't have her figure, anyway. I wonder how old she is. Moisés opens the door and he smiles at her. It's a nice smile, a kind face. How did he know Conchita was walking her dog? He nods, says something, offers a wider smile to Conchita, and closes the door. Conchita looks up to the sky. Her lips move like she's saying something, but to whom? The dog tugs at the leash, wants to continue their walk. Conchita looks down, smiles, and allows her dog to lead the way. I know Moisés misses Carmela. Would I miss Rigoberto? I don't know. My eyes hurt. I need to sit for a while.

Sofia told me a joke yesterday as we drove to school. She said, Mamá, what kind of berries do ghosts like? I gave her my best expectant face and asked, What kind, mija? Already giggling, she barely got out the answer: boo-berries! And she laughed and laughed. A laugh that sounded so ridiculously young and joyful with the discovery of funny words, sentences, ideas. A laugh that doesn't yet know the disappointment of choosing the wrong man to marry. Of feeling foolish for letting a little charm blind you to what was really there all along and plain to any of your friends. So clear that your own mother who believes almost any man can make a good husband could sense it within a minute of meeting Rigoberto. And you said yes to him even though your mother carried through with her threat to boycott the wedding. Sofia hasn't experienced such things and hopefully never will. Oh God. I don't know what she's experiencing right now. I can't let myself think of it. It's too much.

◩

Sofia holds up her bowl so the man can see that she's finished her food.

"Good girl!" he says, patting her shoulder. "That's my good girl."

Sofia puts the bowl down. She remembers how her father told her about the monster of the night that he called el cucuy. He said that el cucuy can appear in any shape and only went after little children who didn't listen to their parents. So what did she do to get caught by el cucuy? Sofia thinks and thinks. And then finally she remembers: She didn't make her bed every morning like she was supposed to. So now el cucuy has her. But for how long?

The man takes the bowl to the sink and splashes water into it. He turns suddenly.

"Oh, did you need more milk?" he asks, noticing that Sofia's glass is empty.

Sofia is too afraid not to nod yes. The man walks over to the refrigerator and looks in.

"Oh, dear," he says.

Sofia turns to the man. He's holding a milk carton and shaking his head back and forth. He taps the carton a little, making a hollow sound, closes the refrigerator, and then tosses the carton into a trash can under the sink.

"We're low on everything," he says dramatically. "And there's no milk left at all. At all, at all, at all."

Sofia shivers but she isn't cold. The man stands by the sink and thinks.

"Well, I think I need to make a little trip to the store."

Sofia looks up. She hopes that she can go with him. That way, she'll have to get her clothes back. The man walks to the bedroom. Sofia sits quietly. When the man returns, he's wearing big, black shoes and a blue sweater. But all he carries in his hand is a set of keys. He squats by Sofia so they're eye-to-eye.

"I'll be back in a few minutes," he says as he pats Sofia's head. "You be a good girl and I'll bring you something special. Okay?"

Sofia nods. The man leaves. Sofia listens to him lock the front door from the other side, get into a car, start it, and drive off. She counts to ten before getting up and running to the window. Sofia pulls aside the curtains and sees a woman across the street walking a thin, gray dog. She recognizes the woman. Who is she? Sofia's mother talks to her sometimes at the market. Sofia likes how this woman dresses with all kinds of bright, happy colors. The woman has let Sofia pet her dog a few times, too. What is the dog's name? Yes! Sarkis! A funny name for a smart, sweet dog. Sofia watches as Sarkis stops and lifts a leg near a large tree whose roots have made the sidewalk rise up at a seam, making it both a tripping hazard and a wonderful ramp to ride a bicycle over. The woman looks up, trying to give her dog a little privacy. And then it happens: The woman glances at the window, blinks, and then squints. Sofia suddenly realizes that she's naked, the blanket in a pile at her feet. The woman's mouth falls open and she says something but Sofia can't hear through the glass. Sofia grabs the blanket and pulls it around her shoulders. And then Sofia decides to do something: She waves to the woman. The woman tugs at Sarkis's leash and starts to call to Sofia. She starts to cross the street. Sofia shivers even more; her teeth chatter. Sarkis stops peeing at the tree, looks up toward Sofia, and lets out one, two, then three sharp yaps.

Sofia wonders if she's in trouble but she stays put, staring at the woman. What is her name? The woman is now at the window, tapping, calling Sofia by her name. Sofia touches the window. It's cold but it feels solid. The woman's tapping makes Sofia's hand vibrate just a bit.

◻

I remember when the doctor first showed me Sofia, holding her up like a magnificent Thanksgiving turkey. After almost twenty-four hours of labor, I had nothing left to give. But there was this little face, red and scrunched up. My baby. And I remember Rigoberto dressed in his hospital greens, a mask pulled tightly over his face. He nodded, his eyes glistening, and I knew there was a huge grin under that mask. I thought that no one could steal this happiness from us. I wondered what Sofia would be like when she developed a personality. Would she love us? How would she adjust to this world? Can she have a good life? Now as I wait here by the phone, the questions aren't much different. Not really.

BELÉN

Belén stumbled and fell hard on her knees in the middle of the dirt road. A chicken clucked in front of her and didn't seem to care that this fifteen-year-old girl's dress was ripped in three places and that dried blood mixed with bits of straw and grime covered her thin legs. Belén knew this stupid chicken. It sported a heart-shaped spot on its left wing and had escaped her uncle's coop three months ago. Tío Normando believed that this unnatural mancha was a bad sign so he didn't bother looking for the bird. Besides, ever since its disappearance, his other chickens gave more eggs than ever before. Now, Belén discerned that the fugitive chicken had grown skinny, filthy, and ragged but the heart shape miraculously maintained its rich, brown shimmer.

"Get away from me," said Belén.

The chicken stopped, cocked its head to the left and then to the right, blinked four times at Belén, and then clucked its way to the other side of the road.

"Stupid chicken."

Belén slowly got to her feet. Her groin hurt but at least the blood had stopped dripping out of her. The sun began to set, filling the sky with brilliant reds and purples. She needed to get home before dark. Belén only had another half mile to go but the pain kept her from moving any faster than a shuffle. Her parents would be angry. But Belén could do nothing to avoid the inevitable screaming from her mother, slap from her father.

"Stupid chicken," she muttered again as she hobbled forward.

As Belén got closer to home, the light emanating from the other homes helped to illuminate the way. These structures could not compare with the one her father had built—most were nothing more than wooden shacks with tar-paper roofs—but they made Belén feel safer as if they stood sentry just for her.

By the time Belén could see the silhouette of her house, the day's heat had dissipated and a chill began to creep into her bones. She smacked her lips and tried to make saliva but couldn't. Belén shivered and thought how magnificent a drink of water would feel right then. Something so simple, so perfect. She closed her eyes and imagined the water on her lips and tongue, and then slaking her parched throat. She'd let some dribble down her chin and then she'd swallow a little and then gulp the rest all at once. That was her plan once she got home if she could stay awake.

Her feet seemed to sink into the dusty road, deeper with each step. Belén heard an owl hoot-hoot-hoot and then a woman's voice—was it her mother?—call her name. She tried to answer but her lips were now sealed dry and tight. And as she fell toward the voice that called her name, Belén believed that she would land safely on her mattress so that she could enjoy a long nap and save that cool drink of water for when she awoke.

◩

"Something like this wouldn't have happened when Cárdenas was president!"

Belén recognized her father's familiar rant against President Manuel Ávila Camacho. Even though he spoke angrily, the sound of her father's voice comforted Belén. She kept her eyes closed and enjoyed the soft mattress.

"Why does it always come down to politics?"

That was tío Normando. Oh! Belén should tell him that she saw his stupid runaway chicken today but she couldn't bring herself to stir or even open her eyes.

"Because politics is everything," said her father, barely controlling his voice. "Politics has turned Mexico into Roosevelt's bitch, that's why. Our good men are moving north to work the fields so Roosevelt can send his men to fight Hitler."

"So?"

"So, because of politics, our daughters can't walk freely in this town without being molested by some stranger who feels that he can swoop down and take what he wants."

"Who said it was a stranger?"

Silence. Just the sound of four people breathing somewhere above her.

And then, slowly: "Because anyone who knows she's my daughter would know that I'd kill him for this."

This last comment from her father sent a shiver through Belén's entire body. Her eyes fluttered uncontrollably, and she coughed.

"She's awake!" Belén heard her mother yell.

Adolfo ran to his daughter but stopped short of touching her. He turned to his wife.

"Mónica, wipe her forehead with a wet cloth," he said.

Mónica complied. The cool dampness refreshed Belén. She opened her eyes and looked at the concerned faces that encircled her.

"Mija," said Mónica. But she couldn't get another word out so she continued to wipe her daughter's forehead and cheeks.

Adolfo came a step closer.

"Who did this to you?" he said.

"Not now," pleaded Mónica.

"Now," said Adolfo. "Was it a stranger or someone you knew?"

Belén thought of that chicken, the one her tío Normando didn't miss at all. But she figured he would be amused by her telling of their meeting earlier on the dirt road where she fell. That stupid chicken looked so ridiculous and skinny and ragged. Yes, that would make her tío laugh his special, deep laugh. ¡Ay! He was so handsome! Her mother was always saying that some lucky girl would steal his heart away. Why couldn't it be Belén? She needed to tell him about the chicken so he could see how clever and funny and observant she was even though she was only a girl and he was a grown man.

"Tío," Belén began, but her throat caught and she broke into a coughing jag.

"Who?" howled Adolfo.

Mónica let out a gasp. She and Adolfo turned to Normando.

"You don't think . . . ," Normando stammered. "Hermano, that's crazy."

Belén gained control of her voice and wanted to tell her uncle about the stupid chicken.

"Tío," she said again, but before she could say anything else, her father leapt across the room and pounced on Normando.

Mónica screamed, "Esposo, it's not possible!"

Normando slipped from his brother's grip. Adolfo stumbled on his own feet and reached for the small wooden table that still held their supper's dirty dishes. The table stuttered and then gave way under Adolfo's weight, collapsing and coming down in a crash that made Belén's ears ring. Normando took advantage of Adolfo's confusion to scamper to the door and rush from the house. Adolfo finally got to his feet.

"I will kill him," he said as he wiped beans and rice from his shirt and pants.

"Why?" asked Belén. "He's my tío."

Mónica let out a whimper.

Adolfo shook his head. "No need to protect him, mija. Brother or not, he will pay for what he did to you."

All Belén could say was: "Tío."

Her parents looked at each other and sighed.

■

Belén's uncle was many things but he wasn't one who took unnecessary risks and he knew too well his older brother's temper. It didn't matter that Normando had not touched his niece or that he secretly desired men instead of women; it was not possible to calm Adolfo. So, that night, Normando disappeared into the darkness. No one knew where he went, though several neighbors saw him gather a few things from his shack, unlock the chicken coop, saddle a horse, and head north. When Adolfo showed up later that night with a loaded rifle, he was met by a dark, empty house and clucking chickens roaming happily in the yard. Six months later, rumors made it back that Normando had sold his horse when he reached Ciudad Juárez and then he crossed the border, eventually settling in El Paso, maybe for good. But no matter. Normando was out of Belén's life so he might as well have been killed by her father.

During those six months of Normando's absence, Belén's belly grew. At first, her mother tried to hide it by making dresses one, two, and then three sizes too big for her daughter. But just when their neighbors started to spread chisme about this unmarried girl's apparent condition, Belén awoke one night drenched in her own blood. The doctor from the Instituto Mexicano de Seguro Social came to finish what nature had started and *poof!*—no more pregnancy, no more gossip. Belén wept at the death of her baby girl, so tiny, so perfect, but without a chance. Mónica tried to comfort her daughter with promises of future babies but within the sanctity of marriage, blessed by the Church, as it should be.

"It's God's plan, mija," said Mónica as she braided Belén's long, sleek hair.

Belén nodded because her mother would know such things. She herself had lost five babies—two before and three after Belén—and had long accepted such deaths as part of a sacred plan. God let many seemingly evil things happen because that was His way. God even let Adolfo confuse what Belén was trying to say to Normando and through such confusion, her favorite tío had to flee for his life. In fact, God later told Belén in a dream that she shouldn't even bother setting the record straight.

"What's done is done," said God.

At least Belén believed that it was God despite the fact that He took the form of that stupid runaway chicken.

"And besides," God added with a cluck, "the identity of the true perpetrators must be kept secret."

"Why?" Belén asked God.

With another cluck, God said: "Because it is part of my plan."

Belén could do nothing but accept God's pronouncement though she did feel a bit odd each time her mother served chicken posole or chicken with rice.

But she figured if she could eat the body of Christ at Mass, she wouldn't be punished if she ate chicken in all of its delectable manifestations.

The next year, Belén started to fill out the oversized dresses her mother had made to hide the pregnancy. Her legs were no longer skinny but had become round and muscular, burned a deep brown from her constant running through the fields. And her bosom—well, something had to be done!—so Mónica bought two sturdy brassieres when they made a special trip to the Federal District. But what surprised her most about Belén was not her rapid development (for this had happened to Mónica suddenly in her sixteenth year as well), but her daughter's remarkable good nature and cheerfulness despite that horrible event of the year before. Ah, no matter. That was all in the past and best forgotten. No doubt Belén will find a good man, marry, and bring Mónica an armload of fat, squirming, happy grandchildren.

But gracias a Díos Mónica never learned that her daughter started slipping out of the house at night to meet Francisco, the young butcher who lived down the road. While Francisco fell in love with this wild young woman, all Belén tried to do was fill a hole that could never be filled. Those trysts ended after a few weeks—the butcher's heart torn to pieces—and Belén grew hungry for something else.

▣

One morning as Belén walked to the mercado for her mother, she decided to take the long way so that she'd pass by her tío's abandoned shack. As Belén approached the tiny structure, she squinted and imagined seeing Normando puttering around the front yard, tending the coop, whistling a happy tune. She marveled at the power of her imagination because she could almost see him there, stooping and picking something up, standing again and taking a puff on a fat cigarette—but her uncle didn't smoke! Belén's eyes popped wide and she froze. Could it be him? Was he back from El Paso with a new smoking habit? She broke into a trot. It was a man, a young man. Could it be Normando?

But as she approached, Belén could see that he clearly was not her tío. Unlike Normando, this man kept his hair cropped close to his skull, and he stood at least six inches shorter than her tío. His face and forearms gleamed a smooth and hairless bronze. So unlike Normando, who boasted a large mustache, hairy arms, and fair skin; he'd always asserted that he and his brother had much more Spanish blood than Indian, something Adolfo confirmed with well-preserved family photographs of Belén's grandparents.

On the other hand, this stranger reminded Belén of the indios who lived in the hills and spoke their ancient language instead of Spanish. A few worked at the Velasco ranch with her father but the boss gave them the dirtiest, worst-paying jobs available. And they wore their traditional clothing and sandals, which did nothing but separate them even further from the town's social fabric. But this indio, he was different. He wore a plaid work shirt with sleeves rolled up to his elbows, jeans, and pointy-toed boots. The man looked up and caught Belén's eye. She stopped, blinked, and stood immobile, five yards away, not knowing what to do or say.

"Señorita," he said with a polite nod.

Belén blinked again.

"Do you speak Spanish?" asked the man.

Belén nodded. She coughed and regained some composure.

"Why do you live here?" she finally asked.

The man laughed and took a long drag from his fat cigarette.

"To protect me from the heat, the cold, the rain," he said.

Belén took a few steps closer and then stopped.

"No," she said, impatient with this stranger. "Why *this* house?"

"I moved from Cuernavaca," the man said while maintaining his calm demeanor. "Now I work at the Velasco ranch. I needed a place to stay so I rented this humble home."

"From my father," blurted Belén, more as an accusation than statement of fact.

The man smiled, revealing straight teeth.

"I see the resemblance," he said.

They stood for a moment in silence, sizing up each other. If it weren't for his boot heels, Belén estimated that they would stand eye-to-eye if she came right up to him. The man kept his cigarette tucked in the left corner of his mouth, making his left eye squint from the smoke. Finally, Belén walked up to him.

"May I have one?" she said, pointing to the man's cigarette.

The man nodded, pulled out a small bag of tobacco and a small, square piece of paper from his shirt pocket, and started to pour.

"Make it fat like yours."

The man chuckled and added more tobacco. He returned the bag to his shirt pocket, gingerly licked one edge of the paper, and rolled a neat but bulging cigarette. He presented it to Belén with a flourish and a bow. She took it, put it between her lips, and leaned into the man. He lit it with the glowing tip of his cigarette.

"You need to draw on it," he said.

And she did. Belén puffed away for a few moments without grimacing or coughing.

"Very nice," she said. "I like it."

Without another word, Belén walked past the man and entered the shack. The man followed. When he entered, he found the girl sitting on his cot.

"Close the door," she said.

"But your father . . . "

"Don't worry about him."

"But you don't even know my name."

Belén dropped the cigarette into a glass of water that sat on the nightstand. It sizzled, making a sound that pleased her. She slowly slipped off one shoe, then the other.

"I'm waiting," she said.

"For what?"

"For your name."

"Celso."

"Good. Now close the door, Celso."

He stood motionless, thinking about this order coming from such a young, beautiful woman.

"I'm not asking again," said Belén.

After a moment, Celso nodded and then obliged.

Adolfo and Mónica could hardly object to the engagement of their daughter to Celso. After what had happened to Belén, they were lucky that any man would want to marry her. Adolfo was far from happy with Celso's deep-brown coloring and his indio features, but at least he was a hard worker, spoke perfect Spanish along with his native tongue, and abstained from alcohol. True, Adolfo's future grandchildren had a fifty-fifty chance of looking like indios, but he knew that worse things happened in life. He also knew that he could trust this indio, which, in this world, accounted for much. Despite his temper, Adolfo was more or less a pragmatist.

Seven months after the wedding, Belén gave birth to a chubby girl whose skin color seemed to be a perfect blend of her parents' shadings. Adolfo sighed in relief when he saw the baby: Though darker than his family, she possessed Spanish features that would make her life easier. Mónica paid no attention to such things. She simply thanked God in all His glory that this baby was as healthy as can be. Belén and Celso named her Concepción but they liked calling her "Conchita." And Belén almost forgot what had happened to her when she was fifteen. Now as a mature woman of seventeen years, she could get on with her life as a mother and wife. Her new husband tore down the old shack and built a larger, new home for his family. Belén believed that her life was on a perfect road, free of the past.

But the past has a way of finding us no matter how we try to hide from it. One night as Celso and the baby snored in unison, Normando appeared to Belén in a dream.

"Oh, Tío," she said to him. "I've missed you so much. Will you ever come home?"

Normando slowly shook his head. This filled Belén with such grief that she began to weep in her sleep. She woke to Celso's strong embrace.

"Mi amor," he said as he pulled Belén close. "Why do you cry?"

But she didn't answer. Within moments, Celso was asleep and his bride hoped that Normando would visit her dreams again. And he did. The next night, as she slept, Normando appeared, but this time he sat at a wooden table holding the runaway chicken in his lap. The chicken was no longer scrawny and dirty. Instead, it was plump and displayed abundant, healthy feathers. That heart-shaped spot looked as if it had grown in both size and brilliance. Normando ran his right palm over the chicken's puffed-out breast and cooed softly to keep the bird calm.

"So," said Belén, "you finally found your bird."

"Yes, she's been waiting for me."

"I thought you were happy to see her go."

"No," said Normando between coos. "I believed that this mancha was bad luck but I always missed her."

Her uncle seemed so content holding the chicken. That bird gave him peace. Belén suddenly felt a pang of guilt for calling it stupid. But wait! Hadn't God spoken to her through this chicken? And here was tío Normando holding God on his lap and cooing to Him.

"Does God want you to do that?" she asked.

"Why wouldn't God want me to hold my chicken?"

"Because God spoke to me through that bird."

Normando's head popped up, a grin spread across his face, and he let out a chuckle.

"My, this is a special chicken," he said and continued to pet the bird.

Belén shifted from one foot to the other.

"What did God say to you through my chicken?"

Belén opened her mouth but then stopped short.

"What did He say to you?" he pressed.

With the question, Belén's mind fell back to the day of the rape. There were two men, men she knew by reputation because of who their fathers were. And God had told her not to divulge their identity, not to set the record straight. And the more she thought about it, the more Belén realized that He was right. If her father had learned the truth, he would have killed these men. And their fathers would have retaliated ruthlessly, no doubt.

"Not much," she finally answered.

"Well, if God went through the trouble of appearing in your dream, I imagine that He'd have something important to say, ¿no?"

Before she could answer, Belén woke to Conchita's wailing. She opened her eyes and saw Celso fully dressed for work, holding their baby.

"She's hungry," said Celso.

"Why didn't you wake me earlier?"

"I thought that I could calm her but I don't have what she needs," he said as he handed the baby to Belén, who quickly put Conchita to her breast. "You looked so peaceful."

The room grew quiet except for the baby's happy suckling sounds.

"Oh?" she asked, feeling her face turn red.

"You were even smiling much of the time except just before you woke," he said.

Belén looked down at Conchita.

"She's beautiful, like you," said Celso.

Belén looked up.

"What's wrong?" he asked.

Belén smiled. Celso leaned down to kiss his wife and touch the baby's puffing cheeks.

"Must go," he said.

In a moment, Belén was alone with her memories of Normando as Conchita fed happily at her breast.

◨

"I've been waiting for you."

Again, in her dream, she found Normando sitting at that little wooden table, holding the chicken. Belén sat down across from him and the bird.

"Do you wait all day while I'm awake?" she asked, truly puzzled.

"In a way," he said, looking thoughtful.

Belén hesitated with her next question, but she had to know: "Are you dead?"

The chicken clucked loudly, flapped its stubby wings, and jumped out of Normando's hands.

"There, you've upset her," said Normando in mock concern.

"Lo siento."

"No matter," he said. And then he paused before answering: "Yes, I am now a spirit."

Belén lost her breath. Normando reached over and stroked her arm in the same gentle way he had been petting the chicken.

"I'm fine," he said. "No more worries."

The chicken pecked at the ground, not wanting to move too far from Normando.

"How did you die?"

"My brother kept his promise."

"No!"

Normando smiled. "I would have done the same."

"But that's not the point," she said. "You never touched me."

Normando nodded in agreement. The chicken came close to his feet and pecked near the toes of its master's shiny boots. Normando reached down with a little grunt and returned the chicken to his lap. The bird clucked contentedly and gave Belén a look that seemed to say: *Ha, ha! He's mine!*

"I must go," she said, standing.

"Of course," agreed Normando.

Belén hesitated for a moment, took a deep breath, leaned down, and kissed her uncle on his cheek. The chicken clucked loudly and flapped its wings. Belén woke to Conchita's hungry cry.

Later that day, Belén set out to the mercado as her mother watched the baby. Normally this was her time to chat and share chisme with the other women of the town. But today, as she haggled halfheartedly with the vendors, Belén was in no mood to gossip. She merely nodded to her female friends or, when forced to, offered nothing more than one- or two-word answers to questions about Conchita and Celso. As she walked home, bags heavy with meat, cheeses, and fruit, Belén's thoughts were gripped by Normando's revelation. Deep in her heart, she'd suspected it, but to be told that her father had killed his own brother based on a misunderstanding filled Belén with an almost paralyzing guilt. She needed to talk to her uncle further about all this, but she'd have to wait until bedtime.

Belén stopped under a tree to rest. She rolled a fat cigarette as Celso had taught her. Belén's mother thought smoking was unladylike. But her father was, despite himself, a bit impressed by his daughter's talent at rolling loose tobacco. As Belén smoked, she let her eyes wander. She took great pleasure in this portion of the road between home and the mercado. The town's pine trees were thickest here, mostly standing in clusters of five or six. On either side of the dirt road, thick grasses grew tall and covered the ground like a thick fur all the way to the foot of the mountains to the east. For reasons she couldn't fathom, the townspeople hadn't built houses here. Belén would, if she could, move her home to this spot. As she pondered the possibility of this, she noticed something moving along the road. She squinted. Some kind of small animal, she figured. Belén puffed on her cigarette, keeping her eyes on the creature's slow but steady progress.

"Ay Díos," she whispered when she realized what approached her.

Belén took one last drag on the cigarette, ground it into the dirt, picked up the bags, and resumed her trek back home realizing that she would soon come upon Normando's runaway chicken. Unlike the bird of her dreams, this chicken was as skinny and grimy as she'd last encountered it. Belén assumed that the bird had died and kept Normando company but she could now see that this, indeed, was the bird with the heart-shaped mancha on its wing.

As they approached each other, Belén realized that the chicken had been clucking softly to itself. The bird suddenly became mute when it noticed the girl but it kept moving forward, though warily. Soon they stood toe-to-toe. The chicken seemed to mock Belén by its refusal to be frightened off the road. How could Normando care for such a spiteful creature? she thought. Perhaps her tío could see the good in it. With that idea taking root in her mind, Belén reached down to touch the heart-shaped mancha, which still maintained its deep-brown luster despite the rather mangy feathers that surrounded it. The chicken eyed Belén's advancing hand suspiciously.

"Good bird," she cooed as her hand drew closer.

The chicken suddenly blinked wildly. As Belén's hand came within an inch of the mancha, the bird emitted a loud cluck, pulled its ragged head back, and then plunged its cracked but sharp beak into the back of the girl's hand. Belén yelped, stood, swung her right leg back, and kicked the chicken with all her strength. The bird let out a bizarre, muffled cackle as it sailed through the air, over a clump of bushes, and directly into a large pine. The chicken bounced off the tree, dislodging a bit of bark upon impact, and finally plopped upon the soft grass, motionless.

"¡Ay!" Belén exclaimed, shocked by her violent reaction.

She ran to the chicken, hoping that it was merely stunned and nothing more. But the unnatural angle of the bird's scrawny neck drained all hope from Belén.

"Oh, what will Normando say?" she whimpered as she fell to her knees.

And then she remembered that God had spoken to her through this bird. Belén knew that she had to do something to show respect for this life she'd taken. She found a sharp branch, snapped it in half, and used it to dig a small grave at the base of the pine. Belén couldn't bring herself to touch the chicken so she gently nudged it with her foot to the edge of the miniature grave and then let the bird fall gently to the bottom. She kneeled and filled the hole with dirt, patting it as flat as possible. Belén stood, solemnly hung her head, and said a prayer. After a few moments of sacred contemplation, she picked up the bags of food and resumed the walk home.

Throughout the rest of the day, Belén clung to the hope that the chicken would be in her dream as usual, comforting her tío. And to her thinking, now that the bird was as dead as Normando, there should be no reason why it wouldn't be there. However, that night when Belén went into her dream, Normando sat at his usual place but his lap and hands were empty, the chicken nowhere in sight. Did he know what had happened? She approached slowly then sat across from her uncle. Normando stared at his empty hands, which rested limply in his lap.

"Tío," said Belén as softly as possible, "how are you?"

"I have something to tell you," he said without looking up.

"I'm sorry," she said.

Normando lifted his head and met his niece's moist eyes.

"No, I'm the one who is sorry for what I'm about to reveal."

Confusion rolled over Belén in waves.

"It's time for you to know," continued Normando.

"What?" was all she could say.

"The identity of the man who took my life."

Belén's confusion grew deeper. She already knew, didn't she? It was her father who had killed Normando.

"But I know," she said. "I've accepted that. It's been easier because I can see you in my dreams."

Normando shook his head. "My brother was indeed responsible for my death, that is true."

"But?"

Normando turned away, shifted in his chair, and coughed. They sat in silence. Suddenly, Normando's eyes widened, a smile spread across his face, and he raised his hands.

"My little bird!" he exclaimed.

Sure enough, the chicken slowly made its way toward Normando, clucking softly, and casting a glance at its murderer periodically. Belén blushed and sighed deeply. She watched as the bird finally made it to Normando's feet. He reached down and placed the chicken onto his lap.

"Yes," Normando cooed to the bird, "rest right here."

To Belén's surprise, the chicken didn't look any worse for its death. In fact, it appeared to have grown plumper and even healthier than the last time she'd seen it in her dream.

"Tío," she said, attempting to hide her annoyance with this intrusion and forgetting her own guilt. "What is it that you want to tell me?"

Normando looked up, still smiling with the joy his chicken gave him. "My brother hired a man to kill me."

Belén fell back in her chair. She could easily imagine her father's anger leading to violence, especially when it came to harm visited upon his family. But a cold-blooded, planned murder with payment made to complete the job?

"This can't be!" she screamed, standing up so quickly that her chair teetered back and rocked until it steadied on its own.

"Why would I lie?"

Belén thought for a moment. Of course he was right: There was no reason to lie to his niece. She pulled the chair back into place and sat, defeated.

"Little one," said Normando. "In the end, it doesn't matter."

"Then why are you telling me this?"

"Because sometimes the truth will teach us something about ourselves."

The chicken clucked in agreement. Many questions came to Belén's mind. But Normando knew this.

"You may ask me only one," he said.

"But . . . "

"Lo siento," said Normando. "Only one."

This agitated Belén. She vowed that when she died and visited the living, she wouldn't be so mysterious. No, she would avoid such games. But at that moment, she had no choice. Belén had to play by her uncle's rules now. She thought for a moment.

"All right," said Belén. "I've chosen one question for you."

"Yes?"

"Who actually killed you?"

"I always knew you were a smart girl," said Normando with a smile.

Belén remained serious, resolute. She crossed her arms tightly across her chest. Normando grew serious as well.

"My brother hired a man, un indio, from Cuernavaca to track me down and . . . "

A shock ran through Belén but she remained quiet to hear everything.

" . . . you know this man."

Belén nodded. For some reason, it made sense to her and she accepted it as she would the color of the morning sky or the smell of her baby's skin. They sat in silence for a long while. Eventually, Normando put the chicken down, smiled, stood, and then walked away. He soon disappeared into the shadows. The bird clucked loudly and then followed its master until it, too, was gone. Belén woke to a kiss on her cheek from Celso.

"Mi amor," he whispered. "Are you all right?"

Belén sat up and rubbed her eyes. Celso didn't rise but kept his head nestled into his pillow.

"Were you having a bad dream?" he asked.

She looked at Celso. The morning sun began to fill the bedroom with a soft light. Conchita snored softly in her crib, which sat in the far corner. Belén strained to see Celso's features clearly. He gently touched her cheek. She wondered how he had killed Normando. Did he use a gun? His bare hands? Belén would never know.

"I'm fine," she said.

Celso pulled her down and she settled into the crook of his arm. Belén listened to her husband's heartbeat. His strong chest rose and fell with each breath. She could feel his limbs grow slack as he drifted back to sleep.

"I'm fine," Belén said again. "I'm fine, mi amor."

9
YAHRZEIT

Julieta looked into the rearview mirror and saw her son staring back at her from his battered Corolla. She didn't know the young man in the passenger seat but without a doubt Rolando sat behind the wheel. Julieta's body buzzed with a shock like the first time she took the twins to Disneyland when they were four years old and she turned for but a second to pay for two Mickey Mouse balloons. Within those moments, Mateo had wandered away from his mother and twin brother. Julieta still remembers her brain being kicked into high gear with a jolt of adrenaline. But the ever-vigilant Rolando pointed through a gaggle of teenagers to his brother, who chatted happily with Cinderella. Now fourteen years later that same vigilant child sat one car length behind her, eyes bulging in recognition and alarm. Julieta pushed Max away from her.

"Ouch!"

"Sorry," said Julieta, confused by the force with which she had pushed this kind, older man away from her.

"I wasn't getting fresh or anything," Max said as he rubbed his left shoulder. "You got quite a right hook there."

"I didn't punch you."

Normally Julieta would have laughed at Max's tendency to talk as if he were some kind of tough guy from the old movies. She knew it was partly an act, partly an honest recognition of his humble beginnings in New York, the sixth of seven children born to Russian immigrants. But under the circumstances, she found no humor in his response. Julieta reminded herself that her conscience was clear. They'd done nothing but enjoy an early dinner together. That was it. But why had she lied to Manuel about her plans for that evening? She certainly had no intention of ruining her marriage by jumping into bed with this gentle, older man. Admittedly, Max was a charmer who made Julieta feel beautiful as he tossed off compliments about her outfits or hair whenever he came into the camera shop. Even Manuel liked Max. He enjoyed the company of this dapper but down-to-earth man—a widower—who knew something about *real* cameras that used *actual* film. Especially one who happily ventured far from his West Los Angeles home to their little shop a few miles from downtown L.A. "A dying art with all this cockamamie digital stuff," Max had said to Manuel when he came in the first time. From that day on, Manuel enjoyed seeing this retired lawyer who knew quality and decried the loss of things that were just fine as is, thank you very much. If it ain't broke, why fix it? Of course Manuel stocked all the new digital products but he kept a corner of one glass case for connoisseurs such as Max, though their numbers dwindled with each passing year.

Julieta returned her eyes to the rearview mirror. No Corolla. No Rolando. Had she really seen him? Or was guilt playing games with her imagination?

"You just passed my street," said Max.

"Darn it!"

"No big deal," he said. "Turn here and we'll sneak up on my house from behind, scare it real good."

Julieta couldn't help herself this time and let out a laugh.

"About that shove, Max," she ventured.

"No, no," said Max, feeling pleased that he could lighten the mood. "It was my fault. I just had such a nice time tonight, I felt close to you. But I was not making a pass." He put his right hand on his heart and added: "Promise."

"I know," Julieta whispered.

They drove in silence until Max said, "That's the old homestead."

"There?"

"Yeah, just pull into the driveway."

Julieta parked but kept her eyes on the house.

"Nice."

"Moving soon," said Max as he undid his seat belt.

"No! From this beautiful place?"

"Yep. My daughter thought that I should simplify my life."

Julieta nodded. Max had mentioned his late wife, Ruth, several times but he always pulled back just a bit and then changed the subject when confronted with questions.

"It's good to simplify," she offered, not knowing how far to go with it. "Life gets complicated and then you don't know which way is up."

"Never a truer word spoken, young lady," Max laughed. "You are both wise and beautiful."

Julieta turned to Max. Max smiled.

"Time to go," he said. "Got things to do."

Julieta couldn't imagine what Max had planned for himself. All he'd said earlier that day was that he wanted to have an early dinner so he could get back home before dark.

"A girlfriend to call?" she teased but immediately regretted it.

Max seemed to think for a moment. And then: "In a sense."

He reached for Julieta's hand, pulled it gently to his lips, and kissed it softly. Julieta blushed.

"Charming evening," he said.

"Yes," said Julieta. "*Beautiful* evening."

Max bowed just a bit, winked, and got out of the car. Julieta didn't drive away until he was safely in his house.

◻

Max entered the kitchen and stood for a moment, taking it in. His cleaning woman, Corina, had come by while he was out, leaving everything gleaming, spotless. Not like Ruth had kept it. She'd believed that good cooking required making a mess. The bigger the mess, the better the food. And though Ruth had been a full-time teacher, she'd refuse Max's offer to hire someone to help around the house. In retirement, despite becoming somewhat frail, she'd been fully capable of maintaining a relatively clean home. It was only in the last year of Ruth's life when the chemo sapped her "oomph"—as she had put it—did this stubborn, loving woman relent and allow Max to hire someone. Corina came highly recommended and proved to be a wonder. Her cooking wasn't all that bad, either. Corina even introduced a few Mexican dishes into the Klein household (Friday became arroz con pollo night) but lightened up on the spices because Ruth's stomach could be a bit iffy after each round of treatment. Corina also loved Windex, Pledge, and anything advertised as possessing maniacal scrubbing bubbles. Max liked to joke that Corina was a chemical engineer. Though Ruth complained that her home had been invaded, Max knew she appreciated not having to worry about such things and that Max would, at the very least, have a clean house and hot meals.

But the one thing about Corina that irritated Max was her penchant for putting away things that he'd set out to use. At that moment, he squinted and scanned the kitchen in search of precisely such an item. Where was it? On Monday, he'd dutifully visited the temple's gift shop and purchased a Yahrzeit candle. Tomorrow was the third anniversary of Ruth's death and he wanted to light the candle at sunset tonight. Max wasn't particularly observant but it wouldn't seem right not to do this in Ruth's memory and in preparation for his trip to the cemetery tomorrow.

Max went from cabinet to cabinet but couldn't find the candle. Where would I put it if I were Corina? he thought. But this didn't help because he knew there was no way he could ever comprehend how Corina approached her vocation. He looked out the kitchen window. The setting sun threw out spectacular reds and yellows. Ruth would have appreciated it.

"Damn it," he said, ready to give up.

But then Max remembered something. He trotted to the study and searched through his desk. Ah! A Yom HaShoah candle from the Federation of Jewish Men's Clubs. He got it in the mail last year as a simple but thoughtful token for Max's donation. The yellow candle sat in a small tin cup emblazoned with the words THE NEXT GENERATION! above a picture of Jewish boys and girls waving the Israeli flag. The healthy youngsters stood in front of a former concentration camp, a physical reminder of the six million Jews who were murdered. This will do, he thought. It looked about the same size as the Yahrzeit candle and would probably burn for the required twenty-four hours. Max trotted back to the kitchen, rummaged through what Ruth had dubbed the tchotchke drawer, and found a book of matches. He set the candle on the counter and lit it. Max stood back and watched the flame rise and fall and then rise again with a small crackle. At times, he wished that he were more observant so that he'd know from memory what prayer to say. But no matter. As he allowed the flame to mesmerize him, Max let his mind wander with thoughts of Ruth. He remembered how his father also outlived his wife. Samuel had lit a Yahrzeit candle for three years but stopped once he remarried. When the fourteen-year-old Max protested, Samuel patiently explained to his son that it would be an insult to his new wife to do so.

"So, Mama didn't exist?" Max had argued.

"It's tradition."

"Who says?"

"Rabbi Weiss."

Max couldn't figure how the wisest man he knew could tell his father to do such a mean thing. But in the end, he didn't blame his father for following tradition though the young Max promised himself that if he lived longer than his wife, he'd light a candle each year regardless of what happened in his romantic life.

Max opened the cabinet near the microwave and pulled out a bottle of Glenfiddich and a tumbler. He paused for a moment before pouring generously. Max lifted the glass to the candle.

"Here's to you, doll."

Max took a sip. He wished his daughters could be in town for tomorrow but Marcie had just started her first trial as lead counsel and couldn't fly in and out of Boston without begging the judge for a two-day recess. Marcie was no beggar and she'd never do anything to prejudice a client's case. And Rachel's sons both had pink eye and felt absolutely miserable. Leaving them behind in Santa Rosa would require a seventy-mile drive to the nearest airport but first adjusting the hard-fought custody schedule she'd hammered out with her ex. Rachel sadly but forcefully demurred and Max understood. Both his daughters had made it to L.A. on the first anniversary for the unveiling of Ruth's headstone and no one could expect them to get back each year. But tomorrow Max would not be alone. Ruth's brother, Aaron, promised to come along. At times, he seemed to take it harder than Max.

Max finished his drink and gingerly placed the tumbler in the spotless sink. He glanced at the candle one more time before turning off the kitchen light. It was too early to go to bed but Max didn't know what else to do. He didn't feel like reading the novel he'd started. Too depressing. Max wandered about the house searching for something to do until finally ending up in the den. He flipped through various channels for a minute but grew annoyed at how much dreck there was on TV even though cable gave him endless choices. He finally settled on a John Garfield movie that he'd seen many times before but at least it was quality all the way. Garfield. Hah! Ruth had liked to remind Max that wonderful actors such as Garfield, Danny Kaye, Edward G. Robinson, and Paul Muni were originally Julius Garfinkle, David Kaminsky, Emmanuel Goldenberg, and Muni Weisenfreund. But the public wouldn't pay for pictures with such Jewish names headlining so the studios and agents forced "safe" monikers on them. Ruth had gloried in the changing times when it became more acceptable for Jews in show business to be themselves. Art Garfunkel! Barbra Streisand! Steven Spielberg! Though she'd been quite annoyed when she learned that Bob Dylan was born Robert Zimmerman. Of all the people who should have been true to himself! But Ruth didn't care for his music anyway unless sung by someone else like Joan Baez. Now, *she* had a voice.

He watched as John Garfield got tough with his racketeer brother in glorious black and white. Yes, Max could settle in with a fine movie and then watch the early news. But maybe he was more exhausted than he'd realized: No matter how much Max wanted to stay awake, his eyes fluttered, his breathing slowed. After several valiant attempts to concentrate on the movie, Max gave up and allowed himself to drift slowly into a soft, inevitable slumber.

And then there Max sits, in Julieta's Lexus, driving on Wilshire Boulevard, having a grand chat with this lovely woman. But in his dream, Max possesses great bravery: He fearlessly leans close to Julieta knowing that she will not push him away. Max's heart fills with both tranquility and exhilaration. And in his dream, there are no messy histories or attachments to worry them, to keep these two healthy, good people from enjoying a little private time together. Complications don't exist. As they drive along, the other cars ease by on either side offering a colorful current through which the Lexus sluices. Max allows his eyes to rest on the smiling Julieta, and then swivels his head to the right to observe the other cars filled with happy people, and then back again to Julieta. "I think I love you," says Max. "I know I love you," Julieta answers without hesitation. "You're the man of my dreams," she adds with a whisper. "And you're all I've ever wanted," Max smiles. He turns to look at the traffic, feeling proud of his heroic assertion of love. The vibrant red and blue and green and silver cars swim by. A brilliant black night sky shrouds the city; the streetlights offer little halos of light. And then an old, black Mercedes comes into view. I know that car, he thinks. Max squints and tries to discern the driver but the Mercedes is two lanes away and other cars keep blocking his view. Finally, the Mercedes changes lanes and pulls even with the Lexus. Max peers into it. Shadow and light take turns filling the black car. Who's driving? Finally, Max's heart leaps as he sees that *he* is driving the Mercedes. And Ruth sits in the passenger seat. They're talking, seriously, to each other. Max stares at them, wondering what he and Ruth are discussing and how he could be in two places at once and how could his beloved dead Ruth be there too. The other Max and the dead Ruth suddenly stop talking. Then she does it: Ruth leans forward and turns her head to the Max in the Lexus. She doesn't frown or scowl or make any face at all. She simply stares at Max, green eyes glittering, catching the moving lights. Nothing more. Max blinks, coughs, tries to remain calm. He turns back to Julieta to see if she's seen the passengers in the Mercedes. But she's smiling, happily oblivious, staring straight ahead as she steers them along Wilshire. Max turns back to the Mercedes. What? He and Ruth no longer sit in the other car. Instead, an older woman now drives all alone. Max doesn't recognize her though she looks familiar. He squints. Where has he seen her before? Suddenly he realizes that the woman resembles Julieta, but older, smaller. And she puffs on a fat, hand-rolled cigarette that begins to fill the Mercedes with billows of white smoke. She turns to Max and frowns. She's saying something to him, plump cigarette bobbing up and down with each word. Max lowers his window. "What are you telling me?" he yells. The woman lowers her window, too, and the smoke is sucked out by the wind. Max yells again: "What did you say?" The woman answers: "The fact of the matter is, if Saddam Hussein were still in power in Iraq, he would be rolling in petrol dollars. Think of the price of oil today. He would have so much money. And he would be seeing the Iranians interested in a nuclear program, he would be seeing the North Koreans developing a nuclear program, and he'd say well why shouldn't he, and he would. So we're fortunate that he's gone." Max shakes his head. "Why are you telling me this?" The woman puffs on her cigarette and then continues: "We're fortunate that the Taliban have been thrown out of Afghanistan and that fifty million people have been liberated. The situation in Iraq is difficult and the violent extremists that are trying to hijack *that* faith have killed an awful lot of Muslims in Iraq and elsewhere around the world."

"What?" Max sat up with a start. "What?" he said again.

Max rubbed his eyes and took a deep breath. Donald Rumsfeld stared back at him from the TV screen making his pronouncements on Iraq. Max fumbled for the remote. He found it under a pillow. Max aimed it at the TV.

"Go to hell," said Max as the screen went dark.

The next morning, Max walked across the carpet of almost perfect lawn toward Ruth's headstone. Aaron promised that he'd be there right on time, but of course he was nowhere to be seen. Aaron liked to joke that he ran on Jewish standard time. Max believed that being late was simply rude and a sign of disrespect. Ruth never kept anyone waiting, that's for sure. He figured this explained Aaron's inability to keep a job or remain married—Max lost count of how many wedding presents he and Ruth had purchased for Aaron over the years. His brother-in-law skated along on little more than a deep anchorman's voice, a head full of curly hair, and a bright, easy smile. With a little hard work, he could have run for office, maintained a marriage, fathered children. But such is life. Ruth had adored her baby brother and that's all that mattered.

Max pulled out a fresh, white handkerchief and wiped the smooth granite around the carved RUTH KLEIN. He stood back and smiled as if he'd just given Ruth a gentle kiss. They both knew, deep down, that she'd be the first to go. While Max had been born in New York, Ruth spent much of her childhood in the camps. After the war, Ruth was the only survivor from her immediate family: Mother, father, two brothers, three sisters, all perished from starvation, abuse, and disease. The gas chamber wasn't needed for Ruth's family. Thank God for her aunt Hannah in Brooklyn who tracked Ruth down with the help of the Central Tracing Bureau and the meticulous records kept by the Nazis. Otherwise Ruth would have spent the rest of her childhood in a miserable displaced persons camp in Austria. Hannah couldn't have children of her own and had been somewhat jealous of her sister, who'd produced so many back in Poland. But now it was her duty to take in Ruth. Hannah's husband, David, couldn't deny Hannah anything and if she wanted to adopt this scrawny concentration-camp girl, then that was that. With Ruth came remarkable luck: Hannah eventually got pregnant and brought Aaron into the world to be Ruth's adoring little brother. But even with their own child now, Hannah and David knew that Ruth was special, a smart girl whose only real failing was her health. Asthma. Brittle bones. All caused by malnutrition from years in the camps, said the doctors. And the New York winters didn't help much. When Ruth and Max met during their sophomore year at Brooklyn College, she told him that she dreamed of moving to California. How could he resist? They married after graduation and moved to Los Angeles where Max began studying law at USC. Ruth's adopted parents and Aaron eventually followed her out west more because they missed Ruth rather than searching for paradise. And over the years, the sunshine and blue skies did help Ruth, some. But they both knew that Max would someday bury her. It was preordained by the Nazis.

"Hey, Maxie."

Max looked up at Aaron's silhouette, the morning sun creating a bright aura around his trim outline. Max squinted and tried to focus on his brother-in-law's eyes. Even though Aaron and Ruth were technically first cousins, they shared the same green eyes. These eyes gave Max a strange sort of comfort, almost as if Ruth hid in her brother's mind to steal a peek at her beloved.

"Hi."

Aaron came to Max's side so they both could look down at Ruth's headstone. "She was a peach," he said to Max.

"Yes, she was."

"No one like her. One of a kind."

"Never a truer word spoken."

Aaron shifted from one foot to the other. He cleared his throat as if he needed to make an announcement. After a moment, Aaron said: "I haven't mentioned this to you, Maxie, because, well, for obvious reasons, but it's hard living in my parents' old house, especially with Ruthie gone. I mean, it makes me realize how really alone I am."

Max didn't know what to say so he didn't respond. Maybe Aaron didn't need a response. Maybe he just needed to say it to someone who would understand. So they stood quietly, both listening to the almost-quiet of the cemetery. A few other people loitered nearby visiting their loved ones. An unseen lawn mower roared in the distance. Aaron sighed, making Max wince at the smell of alcohol. So early to be drinking, even for his brother-in-law. Max looked down and searched for a pebble or small stone. He spotted a nice, smooth one—not too big, not too little. He reached down, emitting a grunt, retrieved the stone, and gently placed it on Ruth's headstone. There. Now people will know that Ruth Klein had family who visited, that she had not been forgotten. Aaron let out another sigh. He reached into his jacket pocket and pulled out a blue, crumpled Kleenex. He slowly opened it as if a mouse hid inside, ready to escape. Max wondered what all this was about. Then he saw: Aaron removed a black, porous stone from the Kleenex, kissed it, and set it next to the one Max had put on the headstone.

"From the Big Island," said Aaron. "Volcanic rock."

"Ah," said Max with a smile. "She loved Hawaii."

"Yes."

Max and Aaron admired the small, black rock as if they both had created it, molded it by hand, using great artistic skill.

"Aaron?"

"Yes?"

Max coughed, rubbed his chin, and wondered what he was going to say. But then it came out: "I've met someone."

Aaron turned to Max. Max immediately regretted saying anything. And then Aaron did something that surprised Max: He gently punched Max in his right shoulder.

"Good for you, Maxie."

"You're not mad?"

Aaron laughed. "Maxie, boy, you're still here on God's good earth. I know you loved Ruthie. You were the goddamned best thing that happened to her, ya know? But you're still breathing," and he waved his hands, palms out, for emphasis.

"But no one could replace Ruth."

"Of course, Maxie."

"But there's a problem."

Aaron grinned. "Hey, they make fine medicines for that."

"No, no, no!" said Max. "Not that."

"I use a little Viagra every so often."

Max grabbed Aaron's shoulders. "No, that's not the problem."

Aaron searched Max's face but he couldn't read an answer there.

Max let his arms fall. "She's married."

Aaron guffawed.

"It's not funny," said Max as he started to walk away.

"Sorry," Aaron said as he followed Max. "It's not funny."

Max stopped and turned to Aaron. "Then why laugh?"

"Because," began Aaron, "I'm usually the one doing stupid things."

"Stupid?"

"Not stupid . . . impulsive, let's say."

Max thought about this. Yes, Aaron was right. He *was* being impulsive. Letting a little friendship turn into love when it really should be enjoyed for what it was.

"Have you done it?" asked Aaron.

"Done what?"

"You know."

Max's face transformed into a horrified mask. "No!"

"Oh," said Aaron. "No harm, no foul, as the late, great Chick Hearn would say."

Max stepped back, rubbed his chin. He'd certainly fantasized many times about making love to Julieta, imagined kissing her, holding her body next to his, whispering into her ear. But to hear Aaron demean such an act was almost too much for Max.

"Look, Maxie, you deserve to be with someone," said Aaron as he drew near. "You're a good guy. A total mensch if there ever was one."

"Thank you," said Max. He realized then that Aaron had meant no harm.

"Hey," said Aaron, perking up. "I have a little joke my buddy Ben told me after shul last week."

"You *still* going to temple?"

"Yeah."

Max blinked but accepted this as true. "Go on."

"Okay, so this old man and woman at a nursing home were sitting in their rocking chairs after lunch."

"Old, like us?"

Aaron laughed. "Old, real old. Like a hundred, okay?"

"Okay, old."

"So, the old guy turns to the woman and says: 'I'll give you fifty bucks if you let me have sex with you.' "

Max crossed his arms. "One of *those* jokes."

"Hear me out, you'll like this one."

"I'll be the judge of that."

"So, the old woman agrees. They go up to her room and do the dirty deed. Afterward, as they're lying back in bed smoking cigarettes, basking in what they just did, the old guy turns to the woman and says: 'If I knew you were a virgin, I'd have offered you a hundred dollars.' The woman turns to the old guy and says: 'If I'd known you could still get it up, I'd have taken off my pantyhose!' "

As the punch line left Aaron's lips, he widened his eyes and grinned in anticipation of Max's response. Max just stood there with no change in his expression, as if Aaron were still leading up to the punchline. Then, ever so slowly, a smile began to form on Max's face and he started to shake. Finally, Max couldn't control himself despite the surroundings: He allowed himself to be lost in loud laughter for nearly a minute. Some of the visitors nearby looked over to see what was going on, but they quickly turned back to their own conversations. Max wiped away tears with his sleeve and then grabbed Aaron's shoulders: "Goddamn you!"

"You're welcome!" said Aaron.

After a moment, Max's arms dropped to his sides.

"Say, are you doing anything tonight? I mean, for dinner?" Max said. "There's this new place on Wilshire, near the old homestead, got a good review in *Los Angeles Magazine*."

"Ah, Maxie, dinner any other night would be fine but tonight I got this Schwarzenegger fund-raiser thing to go to."

Max stifled a laugh.

"I know, I know," said Aaron as he raised his hands, palms outward, near his chest as if to block a punch. "I'm not the political type."

"What's her name?"

"Yeah, you've got my number, Maxie." Aaron dropped his hands and let them dangle in surrender. "Her name is Robin. She's this environmental lawyer who thinks the Terminator is the best thing since sliced bread. Limiting greenhouse gases, smart energy, yada yada."

"How old?"

Aaron grinned. "Old enough."

"Does she have a last name?

Aaron hesitated. Finally: "Robles."

"Nu?"

Aaron stepped back and shook his head. "You, Mr. Liberal, have a problem with me dating a Latina?"

"Ha!"

"What?"

"No, Aaron," Max laughed. "No. The world is just a funny place."

"You bet, Maxie."

Aaron threw his arms open and approached Max. Max preferred not to hug his brother-in-law but what could he do? He opened his arms and allowed Aaron to pull in tight with a full-body embrace. Despite the drinking, Aaron felt lean, strong.

"Love you, Maxie."

"Me, too," said Aaron. "Me, too."

As Max held Aaron, he realized that he could still see Ruth's headstone over Aaron's right shoulder. His own plot—reserved at the same time they bought Ruth's—seemed small, insubstantial. But Max would be there eventually, near his beloved Ruth. He shuddered. Aaron pulled back and searched Max's eyes.

"You okay, Maxie?"

"Oh, sure. You know me. Mr. Tough Guy. You?"

Aaron nodded. He looked at his watch, shook his head. Max nodded back and smiled.

"Gotta go, Maxie. Can I walk you back to your car?"

"Nah, think I'll stay for a bit," said Max, gesturing toward Ruth's headstone.

"Okay, Maxie boy. I understand."

Aaron turned and walked away, slowly placing each foot in front of the other as if the ground would open up any second and swallow him if he weren't careful. Max started toward Ruth's headstone but then stopped after a few steps. Two small birds hopped along the top of the headstone, chirping noisily, heads flicking back and forth. Max wondered if birds could feel happiness, delight, joy. Certainly these seemed bursting with such emotions. Suddenly, one of the birds flitted away up into the full, green leaves of a nearby tree. The other bird hopped around a bit and came near the pebbles that Max and Aaron had placed on the headstone. It pecked at Aaron's little volcanic rock, gave up, and then tried Max's pebble. Satisfied that there was nothing to eat, the bird hopped one more time then flapped its wings, brushing against the pebbles. Max let out a little gasp as his fell from the headstone. The bird flew up into the tree and joined its companion. Max walked to the headstone, picked up the pebble, and returned it to its rightful place.

"You take care, doll," he said. "I'll see you before you know it."

Max turned and tried to get his bearings. Where did he park his car? He squinted and shaded his eyes.

"There it is," he said softly after a few moments.

Max made his way to the parking lot. Before getting into his car, he looked back. The small birds had abandoned the tree and again danced on Ruth's headstone. They chirped excitedly.

"Hope you're having fun," said Max to the birds as he opened his car door and settled in. "Sing your hearts out for my gal."

10

WANT: A SYMPHONY

Los Muertos

The afterlife really began to annoy Belén. True, there were great benefits to take pleasure in such as victory over pain and hunger and fatigue. And she could puff away on her fat, hand-rolled cigarettes without fear of cancer. Visiting with Celso and others was not so bad, either. Here, there were no hurt feelings if you wanted some privacy. Everyone understood. The transgressions from life on Earth also were forgiven. And there were, of course, answers to the many questions that have haunted people for so long: Is there but one, true religion? Why does God allow evil to exist? Does God really care if Notre Dame wins a football game?

And of course there was the great revelation of finally being able to see the face of God—after a lifetime of wondering. But what annoyed Belén was the fact that she still had plenty of free will. Too much, truth be told. She could stay in heaven or wander back down to Earth and observe the living, visit them while they slumbered, assert herself in night visions. Belén knew before she died that spirits liked to stay involved in this way. She'd seen her own late mother, Mónica, once or twice in dreams. One day, after much thought, Belén confronted God about all this.

"Why," she asked, "can't I simply stay here and enjoy eternal peace with Celso and the rest of my dead family and friends?"

"You may certainly do that," answered God. "I'm not stopping you."

"But I feel compelled to come back to Earth from time to time to assist my children," Belén continued as she puffed on her fat cigarette. She blew magnificent, perfect smoke rings that impressed God mightily.

"You may do what you want, my daughter," said God in a patient, loving voice.

Belén noticed that God was both handsome and beautiful at the same time with a countenance that shimmered and undulated and filled her with warmth. God's good looks were distracting. She had to concentrate to stay on point.

"But you know as well as I that if given a choice, I will interfere with the living," said Belén as she puffed more rapidly on her cigarette.

"And your point is?"

Belén marveled at how God could answer like that without sounding one bit snotty. But He could do anything, of course. After a tad more discussion, Belén realized that God wouldn't budge on the rules. She threw her hands up in exasperation. God laughed. Belén cherished His laugh. In fact, it was one of the best things about the afterlife.

"I love you more than you could ever know," said God.

Seeing that God prepared to leave, Belén said: "Please don't go."

"So much to do!" exclaimed God before disappearing.

Belén shrugged. She should have known better than to waste her time trying to argue with God. But since time no longer meant anything, it really didn't matter. Belén looked down to Earth. Her children were more or less sleeping. She squinted. Who was that? Oh, yes. Max Klein. Belén liked his looks and knew that he generally had a good heart. And she'd met his late wife, Ruth, who was the life of the party and quite an intellectual, a philosopher even. What that poor Ruth went through in the camps! Oh, it angered Belén so. But Ruth could talk about such horrible things without getting upset. One of the benefits of the afterlife, of course. In fact, just the other day, they'd had a very nice chat about the many faces of evil.

Belén squinted again: There was Max, fast asleep on his couch, dreaming of Julieta! Shame, shame, shame!

"She's married, you!"

Belén sighed and came down into Max's dream. She liked the car she landed in: soft leather seats, bright gadgets on the dashboard, and a smooth ride. Belén puffed on her cigarette and tried to think. What should I tell this nice, confused old man? Should I scare him witless? She turned to him. Max sat in the other car as Julieta drove. My, this man loves her, doesn't he? Belén thought. This will be rough going. She pondered her options for a moment. What should I say to him? How can I stop this?

Once Upon a Time

En un país muy lejano, there lived a woman of a certain age who owned a camera shop with her husband. She had two healthy sons (identical twins, in fact), who attended a local university. She enjoyed the company of her sister who lived nearby but missed her other sister who still lived in the old country, across the southern border. All in all, the woman believed that she lived a perfectly fine life. But concerns did weigh on her mind. She still could not forget the horror of planes crashing into the World Trade Center, the Pentagon, and that faraway field in Pennsylvania. She became obsessed with the mothers who died or who lost husbands, children, and siblings that day. She always worried about the mothers. And the war in Iraq confused and angered this woman; no matter how hard she reviewed the facts as she knew them, the woman could not see the connection between 9/11 and the war her country waged. The woman kept all of this to herself believing that no one wanted to know this side of her.

One morning, as the woman and her husband tended to their camera shop, a man walked into the store. The woman looked up from what she was doing and smiled. The man smiled back and for a moment simply stared into the woman's eyes. This made her uncomfortable for but a moment, and then she blushed and felt as silly as a young girl. This is an old man, she thought. Trim and well dressed, but old . . . he must be at least seventy—probably older—the woman concluded.

The woman's husband offered a hello and asked how he could be of help. The new customer held up a solid, shiny camera. Can you fix this? he asked as he pointed to it. The husband's eyes widened as did his smile. I haven't seen one of those in many years! he exclaimed.

As her husband happily attended to the customer, the woman watched the two men lose themselves in admiring and discussing the old camera. For reasons she could not understand, the woman wondered at that moment if her husband had ever been unfaithful to her. This thought made a chill go down the woman's spine and she shuddered. In truth, she had nothing to worry about: Her husband had been faithful throughout their marriage despite a temptation or two. But he did keep several secrets from his wife, including the existence of a daughter.

The woman also wondered why she found this stranger so intriguing. She thought that perhaps it was hunger; her breakfast had been too small even for her diet. The woman then thought about the mothers of 9/11 and how they felt each time the images of that horrible day flashed on TV or appeared on the cover of magazines or when President Bush mentioned it in a speech. How could these mothers live with such pain? And she wondered why God let it happen. If everything had a reason, what was the reason for 9/11?

Suddenly, her husband came close and pecked the woman's cheek. Nice old man, he said. And what a wonderful camera, he added.

The woman looked around the shop and realized that the customer had left while she'd been lost in thought. But she knew that she would see him again. The woman knew this as certainly as she knew her own name.

Lunch

"¿Qué va a tomar, señor?"

Manuel looked up at the waitress. She reminded him of his tía Eloisa: all sharp angles, not an ounce of fat, and a bright smile as big as a slice of sandía. But much younger than his tía. Manuel's daughter had suggested this little place on Spring Street, said the food was good and inexpensive. Authentic. Manuel figured it didn't really matter. The point of the lunch was that this would be the first time he and Teresa met in person. The e-mails, exchanged photos, the three phone calls. Those didn't count. So awkward and impersonal, really. What could he ask? How was prison food? Do you intend to keep in touch with your convict friends like La Queenie? No. This was the test. Face-to-face. Eye-to-eye. The waitress hovered, smile straining just a bit, as her customer sat lost in thought, clearly uncertain of what he wanted to eat. She suggested the carnitas plate. Manuel figured that he might as well order. Twenty minutes late. Where is Teresa? He turned to the waitress and nodded.

"¿Y una cerveza?" she asked.

Manuel shook his head, pointed at his water. Beer would not be a good thing to have. Besides, it was a workday, the camera shop had been open for four hours, and he'd have to get back after lunch. The waitress wandered to the back of the restaurant to place the order.

Julieta had reacted better to the news than Manuel ever expected. She did that sometimes: surprise him in such a way that made him fall deeper in love with her. But he wished Julieta had agreed to come. She said, No, you have to do this alone. You have to build this relationship slowly, in baby steps. Julieta was right, as usual.

Ensenada Restaurant began to hum with customers, mostly Mexicans who looked like they worked hard for a living, with their hands. That's how you knew the food was authentic, by the customers. But as the minutes passed and the tables filled, Manuel noticed that there were more and more patrons who looked as if they worked in the nearby law offices, the Reagan State Building a couple of blocks down Spring Street, and the many banks scattered throughout downtown. He observed people of many different shades: black, white, yellow, brown. People who appreciated good food. Manuel figured that if the world ever stopped fighting and hating, it would be because of food. Food was the bridge, the antidote to war, bigotry. How can you hate a culture that produces wonderful things to eat?

Where was she?

Manuel grabbed a tortilla chip and dipped it in salsa. He held the crisp, fried triangle above the bowl and watched as a red droplet hung for a moment before falling back with a small *plop* into the salsa. This was so stupid. Why did he come? He bent his marriage in half, telling Julieta about his secret daughter, agreeing to meet this woman, this half sister to his twin boys. The boys. Los Dos. How will they react? Julieta said to wait on that. Meet Teresa first. See how it goes. But where was she? Manuel popped the tortilla chip into his mouth and crunched loudly.

"¿Papá?"

Manuel looked up. He blinked. This was the first time she'd called him that. She already accepted him as her father. The word sent a shiver through his body.

"Teresa?"

She nodded. Manuel stood and looked at her. Teresa reached out to hug him. Manuel stepped back, bumped the table. He grabbed her hand and shook it gently. She smiled, looked down, and then back up.

"May I sit?"

Manuel pulled a chair out and held it until his daughter settled in. He sat down and kept his eyes on Teresa's hands, which rested in little fists on the table. The waitress brought the plate of carnitas and put it down in front of him.

"That looks wonderful," said Teresa.

Manuel smiled proudly almost as if he'd cooked it. "You want the same?"

Teresa nodded. Manuel lifted his plate and put it before his daughter. He ordered another plate for himself and turned back to Teresa, who sat motionless before the food.

"Please start," he said. "It'll get cold."

She hesitated for a moment.

"Please, I mean it," said Manuel.

Teresa nodded.

"Yes, Papá," she said. "Thank you."

"Cómo no, mija" said Manuel. "Cómo no."

Journalism 101

Interviewer's notes: April 3, 2006. *Women's Facility, State Prison. Prisoner will be brought out soon. Interview with Reyna Escondida, who prefers to go by the name "La Queenie." She's now being escorted through a metal door to a seat across from me. We're separated by thick Plexi or some other kind of unbreakable glass, I'm not certain. I'll find out later, maybe I can use it somehow, as a metaphor for something. She nods to me and picks* *up the receiver on her side. I pick up mine. We chat for a little as I try to set her at ease. But she's nervous, kind of jumpy. Much smaller than I expected. Can't be more than five foot one or two. Thin but pretty. I finally decide to jump right in with the questions I really want answered.*

Interviewer: So, why did you agree to be in this novel?

La Queenie: *This* is a novel?

Interviewer: It says so on the cover.

La Queenie: Don't believe everything you read.

Interviewer: You sound angry.

La Queenie: No, just tired.

Interviewer: Is that all?

La Queenie: You know Teresa's been released?

Interviewer: Yes.

La Queenie: I guess I miss her.

Interviewer: We can do this another time.

La Queenie: She brought out the best in me.

Interviewer: Really, we can reschedule if you need to.

La Queenie: No. It's okay.

Interviewer: Sure?

La Queenie: I've no place else to go. Kind of a captive audience. Why did you choose me to interview?

Interviewer: You seemed like such a good person in chapter 2, even wise. Kind to Teresa, giving her advice, that kind of thing.

La Queenie: But I never really make an appearance in chapter 2.

Interviewer: Right. We meet you through Teresa's letter to her mother.

La Queenie: Do you have a question?

Interviewer: Okay. Like I asked before, why did you agree to be in this novel?

La Queenie: Assuming this is a novel—seems more like a bunch of short stories strung together—but assuming it is, I really didn't have a choice. He made the decision, not me.

Interviewer: Who?

La Queenie: Olivas.

Interviewer: I'm sure that if you'd asked him, he would have given you a choice.

La Queenie: Ha!

Interviewer: Yes, I'm sure of it. He seems very nice.

La Queenie: He's a pendejo.

Interviewer: A what?

La Queenie: Hard to define that word. Not a compliment, let's put it that way.

Interviewer: He's very polite, though. And I'm sure he would have allowed you to opt out of being one of his characters.

La Queenie: Las apariencias engañan.

Interviewer: What?

La Queenie: He's got you fooled.

Interviewer: No . . .

La Queenie: He even has you thinking that this is a novel.

Interviewer: Okay. Let's move to something else.

La Queenie: Look, Olivas invented me, he invented you. He doesn't have to pay us or take care of our medical bills or anything. We're basically slaves. He's like a prison guard. Wait, no, he's worse because at least a prison guard knows her place in life. Olivas thinks he's writing a great novel like *The Hummingbird's Daughter* or *The People of Paper*. He's too much of a baboso to realize that he's no Urrea, Plascencia, Viramontes, Rodríguez, or any one of a number of Gonzálezes.

Interviewer: Who?

La Queenie: Now, those are writers! But even the best got their own issues, as my AA counselor would put it.

Interviewer: What kind of issues?

La Queenie: I get to read a lot here and I've discovered something: All writers live in their own little worlds.

Interviewer: *All* writers?

La Queenie: That's what I said.

Interviewer: Ah, Hempel's paradox.

La Queenie: ¿Cómo? Make sense, lady. I have no idea what you're talking about.

Interviewer: All ravens are black . . .

La Queenie: ¡Ay! You're loca!

Interviewer: Sorry. Not important. Why did you befriend Teresa?

La Queenie: Nice girl.

Interviewer: You gave her advice about family and God.

La Queenie: Is that a question?

Interviewer: No. Just an observation.

La Queenie: How do you know this stuff?

Interviewer: I've been allowed to read the whole manuscript.

La Queenie: Olivas let you?

Interviewer: Yes. But he had to get approval from U of A Press first.

La Queenie: Why can't I read it?

Interviewer: Because it would affect what you do.

La Queenie: That's ridiculous. I'm only in one chapter—as far as I know—and only through a letter. And why wouldn't it affect what you do? Doesn't make sense. You're getting special treatment.

Interviewer: It doesn't matter. Don't get upset.

La Queenie: I do what Olivas makes me do. But I'd like to read the whole book.

Interviewer: It's still in proof form—lots of edits needed. Anyway, not even his wife has read it. I doubt he'd let you have a copy.

La Queenie: But he let you have it.

Interviewer: Research. I had to prepare for this interview.

La Queenie: But you don't exist, except in Olivas's imagination.

Interviewer: No need to attack me. I'm paid to ask questions and I'm trying to be nice and as gentle as possible, considering your circumstances. I mean, I really thought that you were going to be an easy interview. I probably should have chosen Julieta or Conchita or even that child molester in chapter 7.

La Queenie: Go ahead, get a new assignment. I think I'm done. Guard! I'm done with this lady. ¡Ya basta! I want to go back.

Interviewer: Wait. I'm sorry. That was uncalled for. Please don't go.

La Queenie: No. I'm tired. Bye.

Interviewer: Please?

La Queenie: No. And tell Olivas . . .

Interviewer: What?

La Queenie: Nada.

Interviewer: Tell me.

La Queenie: He's not worth the energy.

The Very Selfish Man

Mateo snored loudly, his tiny nose pointed toward the ceiling, the Mickey Mouse balloon hovering above him, still anchored to his wrist by a string. Rolando's balloon had escaped his grasp in Disneyland's parking lot. They'd watched as it rose slowly, those round ears glistening in the moonlight, until the balloon was nothing more than a red fleck and then nothing at all. Now Rolando stared enviously at his twin brother's triumphant rodent, full and tight and safe. He finally looked away and tried to get comfortable. But jealousy and anger consumed him. He wished that Mateo would disappear so that he was the only one. He was fed up with being a twin. Rolando fantasized that Mateo would suddenly inflate with helium and drift up and then out the window, floating farther and farther until no one could see him. This gave Rolando a deep satisfaction but did nothing for his restlessness. He noticed a creaking down the hall by his parents' bedroom. Before he knew it, his father stood at the doorway. "What's wrong, mijo?" Manuel whispered as he opened the door wider.

"Can't sleep."

Manuel came in and sat on the edge of Rolando's bed.

"Sorry your balloon got away."

Rolando grew brave and said: "I wish I was your only son."

Manuel tried to hide his smile. This was normal, he knew. He told Rolando that he'd said almost the same thing about his sister long ago. This surprised the boy.

"Did you tell Abuelito this?" he whispered to his father.

"Oh, yes."

"Did he get mad?"

"Oh, your grandfather was too smart to get mad," said Manuel. "Instead, he told me a story."

Now Rolando grew excited. "A story?"

"And I'll tell it to you if you promise to get to sleep when I'm done."

Rolando nodded. Manuel leaned close and began:

Long ago, at the far end of the pueblo, there lived a very selfish man. Because of his selfishness, he was not a very pleasant person to be around. The people of the pueblo left him to his own devices and tried not to tread on the road that ran by his dilapidated house. Being left alone was the only thing that made this selfish man happy.

How selfish was this man? Well, he was so selfish that he did not even want to share his broken-down old house with his own shadow! So, most days and nights, he kept his windows shut tight with the dusty old curtains closed so that the light of the sun or moon would not shine in and cast his shadow within the house.

But the selfish man could not hide in his house all day. Even he had to eat. So, each morning, he would creep out of his dark and musty house to pick some fruit and gather some vegetables that grew in his yard. One such morning, as he reached for a ripe apple, he heard his front door shut with a loud crack. In a panic, the man ran to the house.

"Who is in there?" he bellowed as he pounded the heavy wooden door with his fist.

"Your shadow!" came the response.

The selfish man's eyes widened in disbelief and fear. Was this a trick? he thought. He had to find out.

"Prove it!" yelled the selfish man.

And what happened next was most remarkable. The voice on the other side of the door proceeded to recite many secret things that only the selfish man could know, such as what the man ate each day, which side he slept on, and how many naps he took. The selfish man could not believe his ears! But the voice had indeed proved that it was the man's shadow.

"May I come in?" asked the selfish man.

There was a long silence. Finally, the small voice answered: "Only if you agree to share your life with me."

The selfish man thought for a moment. How could this be a bad thing? he thought. After all, my shadow has been with me since I was but a baby. Maybe it is time to share this old house.

"Yes," said the selfish man. "You may share my home with me."

The door creaked open. The selfish man looked down and saw his long shadow stretch across the floor of his old house. After the man entered, he opened all the curtains to let in as much sunshine as possible. When the people of the pueblo learned of this, they did not mind walking past the once-dark house. Indeed, if they saw the man sitting on his porch, they would say hello. And the man would offer a loud and happy greeting. And, if they had looked carefully, the people would have seen the man's shadow waving a hearty hello, too.

Rolando's eyes widened. Manuel kissed his son's forehead.

"Now, to sleep, you," he whispered.

Manuel stood, touched Rolando's cheek, and walked out of the room. The boy turned back to the Mickey Mouse balloon. And as he began to get drowsy, Rolando smiled with images of his brother floating far from their home, over rooftops and trees and backyards, never to be seen again.

My Princess

"What's your name?"

Mateo looked up at Cinderella. Her blond hair glistened. She was perfect, thought the boy.

Cinderella bent down, put her white-gloved hands on Mateo's shoulders, and announced to him in a somber voice: "You're a very handsome boy, do you know that?"

Mateo shuddered. How could anyone so beautiful notice him? She was an angel.

"My name is Mateo."

"Maw-teh-oh?" she said. "What kind of name is that?"

Mateo looked into Cinderella's blue eyes. Her blue, satin dress was more brilliant than the afternoon sky. Boys and girls walked past them toward the balloon man. A long line of tired adults and excited children waited nearby to get on the Pirates of the Caribbean ride. Three little birds took excited turns pecking at the top half of an abandoned hamburger bun. Mateo knew then that he loved Cinderella with all of his heart and that they would be married someday and they would have a little house near his parents.

"Did you hear me?" said Cinderella.

Mateo blinked and nodded.

"Well, what kind of name is it, then?" she said, punctuating her query with a little squeeze of the boy's shoulders. "I *really* want to know." Then she added: "*Cinderella* really wants to know."

"Mexican," Mateo finally answered. "I'm named after my uncle who lives in Mexico City."

Cinderella lifted her hands off of the boy's shoulders so fast Mateo wondered if she'd received a shock from him. But he didn't feel anything and those kind of shocks usually happened when he rubbed his feet on the carpet. Cinderella narrowed her eyes, looked left and then right to see if she and the boy were more or less alone. She leaned close to Mateo's ear.

"Mexicans are dirty people," she whispered with a smile.

Mateo held his breath.

"I'm right, aren't I, Maw-teh-oh?" she said, nodding, coaxing.

The boy returned the nod. Now he and Cinderella were nodding together. How could he not? Cinderella wouldn't lie. And besides, Mateo's mother always complained about how dirty he got when he played outside. Sometimes she called him Pig-Pen, just like Charlie Brown's grubby friend. For a moment, they stared at each other in silence. And then their private connection snapped with Mateo's mother's call: "Mateo!"

Julieta trotted to Mateo and Cinderella pulling Rolando and two Mickey Mouse balloons behind her.

"Go to your mommy and brother, you little beaner," whispered Cinderella.

Mateo let his eyes wash over this beauty one more time before turning and running to his mother.

"Don't ever wander!" said Julieta as she hugged Mateo. "Don't you ever do that again! You scared me half to death."

"I'm sorry."

"Why couldn't you wait until we got the balloons?"

"I wanted to talk to Cinderella," said Mateo. "I love her."

Julieta glanced up to look for her son's object of desire. Cinderella strolled several yards away from them, waving at children, smiling a broad smile. Julieta noticed several strands of brown hair peeking out at Cinderella's nape from beneath an otherwise perfect, blond wig. Julieta laughed to herself, wondered how in this land of beaches and surfers they couldn't find a real blond to play the part.

"She *is* beautiful," said Julieta.

Mateo nodded. "Yes," he said. "Very beautiful."

Shopping for a Necktie

I run my fingers across the neatly folded neckties, enjoying the different textures of silk on my skin, letting the designs fill my eyes with color. I'm always best in the fourth week. That's when I feel like I can go out and live a normal life. The first week is the worst. I have no energy, I can't keep food or drink down, the chemo is doing its best to poison the cancer but, in the process, is poisoning me. The second week is a bit better: I can eat some food if it's bland, like toast or crackers or oatmeal. Max makes me drink these chocolate and vanilla drinks—Ensure, Boost, Equaline—silly names, all high in calories and vitamins and protein, for people like me who need to gain weight. By the third week, I'm becoming more myself, but not quite. And then by the fourth week, where I'm at now, I'm the Ruth everyone knows. I can even drink my morning coffee and read the paper with Max just like we've done for so many years. That's my favorite time.

Ah! That's it! That's the tie I'm looking for. I reach across the table to get it before anyone else can—it's one of a kind. I hold it up and against Max's chest.

"That will go perfectly with your gray suit," I say.

Max looks down at me and smiles. He's always been a sharp dresser. Even back in college. But I noticed that some of his color combinations were a bit off. It wasn't until we were engaged that he fessed up to being color-blind. So I told him that I'd be his clothing adviser, forever. He liked that. This necktie I hold up is burgundy with very fine, diagonal black lines running through it. Quite subtle. I'm sure Max sees it as a brown mush.

"Very nice, sweetie," he says.

My Max. My beautiful, handsome, strong Max.

I don't tell him that I'm getting his wardrobe ready for the funeral. I helped him choose the gray suit before I started chemo. And now Max needs a good tie to go with it. But not too nice. This will be the tie that gets cut with scissors at my gravesite the day I'm buried. The rending of garments, grief the Jewish way.

"But do I need another tie?" he asks.

I smile and nod.

"It is nice," he says, relenting. In the old days, before the cancer, we'd have a little more give-and-take, maybe a tiny argument if we had extra energy to expend. But no more. Max gives in on everything now. That's okay. For three weeks each month, I actually appreciate it. But in this fourth month of chemo, I kind of miss the way we used to talk.

"Let's buy it," he says. Max touches the tie, very gently, as if he could break the silk. "Very soft," Max adds.

I move the tie away from Max and let it hang in front of me. It is beautiful. After a moment, I lay the tie on the table, fold it, and set it back at its old spot.

"You have plenty of ties," I say to Max.

"Oh?"

"Yes," I say. "No need to add another one to your bounty."

Max laughs.

"You're the boss," he says.

I smile and nod. Max puts his arm around my shoulders. He almost encases me, my bear of a man. He leads me away from the necktie table, toward the exit.

"I could use some pie," says Max. "And a nice cup of coffee, too."

"That would be perfect," I say. "Perfect."

▣

She's so small now, my Ruth. She was never big but she can't keep the weight on because of the chemotherapy. But right now, she's enjoying this time out with me, searching for a tie. I really don't need one but it makes her happy. Ruth loves to touch the silk, admire the designs. She reaches over to a tie that catches her eye. Her sleeve rides up revealing the small, faded tattoo, that number she refuses to have removed. It's Ruth's private reminder that it could happen again. I was lucky, being here during the war. She doesn't say too much about the camps. Except how she survived because of little things. Like the fact that she could draw. One of the mothers asked Ruth to draw pictures on the walls of the children's barracks. She was able to get some charcoal and drew a meadow with trees and grass and flowers and little critters—a few rabbits, birds, a turtle. An SS guard saw it one morning, stared at it for a long time. Ruth thought she was going to get it for sure. But that guard showed it to the other guards. They were all impressed. They offered her extra bread if she drew pictures for them. One guard wanted his portrait done. He even gave her a set of watercolors to do it. Ruth said she couldn't believe how magnificent the colors were. Ruth did the portrait and the guard loved it. He showed it to the other guards, bragged how handsome he looked. The other guards wanted theirs done, too. Ruth agreed. It kept her busy, took her away from the daily suffering. Sometimes she'd take extra long just to stay inside the warm officers' quarters. But the important part of this story is the bread the guards gave her. Without this extra nourishment, Ruth believes that she would have starved or been too weak to survive what was to come later, before liberation.

"That will go perfectly with your gray suit," Ruth says.

I look down at her and smile. Ruth has always helped me choose my clothes because I'm color-blind. When we got engaged, she said that she'd be my clothing adviser. For as long as she lived. I liked that. But the tie Ruth now holds to my chest looks kind of brown or purple or something. I can't tell. Not very pretty at all. And it has these tiny black lines running through it. A mush to me and my defective vision.

"Very nice, sweetie," I say.

Ruth is lost in thought again. I used to be able to read her mind, almost. But since the cancer, I often can't imagine what she's thinking.

"But do I need another tie?" I ask.

Ruth smiles and nods.

"It is nice," I say. I don't want to argue. We don't have very many good days anymore. Today is a good day.

"Let's buy it," I say. I touch the tie, very gently, to show how interested I am. "Very soft," I add. It is very soft.

Ruth moves the tie away from me and lets it hang in front of her. She's admiring it, humming a little, lost in thought again. After a moment, she lays the tie on the table, folds it, and sets it back at the end of the table.

"You have plenty of ties," she announces.

"Oh?"

"Yes," says Ruth. "No need to add another one to your bounty."

This makes me laugh. "You're the boss," I say.

Ruth smiles and nods. I put my arm around her tiny shoulders. So small, nothing but bones. I lead her away from the necktie table, toward the exit. I'm not certain why we came to Macy's in the first place.

"I could use some pie," I say. "And a nice cup of coffee, too."

"That would be perfect," says Ruth. "Perfect."

How We Live

Just before I was murdered, I'd lain with Federico. The horror of my past, the mistaken belief of my brother that I had raped Belén, my beautiful niece, had fallen away for a short while in the arms of my love. When I'd settled in El Paso,

Federico was the first man I'd dare to speak with for any length of time. I had to be careful for two reasons. First, my brother, Adolfo, was stubborn, relentless—I'd seen these traits repeatedly while growing up—and I had no doubt that my brother would not give up until he was avenged. Second, my secret life with men was always kept wrapped up in my chest, my covert self that, if discovered, could get me killed too.

In El Paso, my situation was almost perfect. Señora Espinoza's boardinghouse for men became my home, a single room all to myself, a bathroom down the hall. She served breakfast and dinner for her men, all seven of us who lived there. I think she liked having us around, the children she and her late husband could never have. The señora seemed most blissful feeding us, inquiring if our beds were comfortable, wondering if we had all that we needed. She was of an indefinite age, her skin smooth and tight due to being very large. I suspect that if she'd been a lean woman, her true years would have been more apparent. In any event, this was my new home and I made the best of it.

After a month or so at the boardinghouse, I'd gotten used to the other men. They were all Mexican, save for one German who'd lived in Guadalajara his whole life until moving to Texas at the age of sixteen. The other men were of an assortment of sizes, ages, and histories. And then there was Federico, ten years my senior, who moved in a week after I did. We noticed each other, above the others, for reasons I can't understand. He listened intently to everything I said, even the silliest comments. One evening, he visited my room to borrow a little tobacco, or so he said. But that visit became the first night we spent together. After that, we had to be very careful, of course, making excuses to visit each other. This was not too unusual because every man in that house needed friendship since they'd left everyone behind in Mexico. Sometimes one would visit the other's room to play cards or listen to Mexican records. Of course, the other men visited putas whenever they had extra money. One or two had real girlfriends. And I had Federico. We had each other. I was happy.

One evening after sharing his bed, I grew restless and wanted to go out and have a drink. Federico just wanted to sleep. So I kissed him and left the boardinghouse. Down the road was a bar that I enjoyed called La Bolsa Chica. Men and women, almost all Mexican, came to eat and drink and dance. I felt like I was at home once I had a few copitas of whiskey. After having more than was wise, I stumbled out of the bar. The street was virtually deserted, an automobile passing every few minutes, two or three inebriated couples walking home. I decided to take a shortcut, down an alley. The dark never scared me. Never, not even when I was a child. And it was in the alley, not two blocks from the boardinghouse, that I encountered a man. He smoked a fat, hand-rolled cigarette, obscenely large. The man seemed harmless enough, lost in thought. But his face became the last I saw, when I was alive.

It took many years for Federico to be with me again. He'd lived a long life, mostly alone, after I was murdered. But after he died, we were reunited. He smiled, said hello, and held me tight in his strong arms. Federico chooses not to visit his loved ones back home. He says he doesn't want to interfere. I personally find this a superior gift, being able to visit those I left behind, a gift that I should not waste. You agree. ¿No?

What We Do When Others Aren't Watching

"So, it is settled," says Adolfo.

Celso sips his beer. The bar is almost empty, a time when most men are working. He looks at the bottles behind the bartender, all the beautiful glass and colorful labels.

"So?" Adolfo says, turning to Celso. "It's a deal?"

Celso looks down at the photograph of the man. "He looks a lot like you."

Adolfo coughs, takes a long drink from his beer. "Yes."

"Who is he?"

"You will have to know anyway, in order to find him in El Paso."

"Well?"

Adolfo pulls out a white envelope. "Here is the first payment," he says. "The second I will give you when you get back. Along with a place to live and a regular job, as you wanted. Though why you'd want to leave Cuernavaca . . . well, that's your choice."

Celso drags the envelope to himself and lifts the flap to see the money. He doesn't count it. Celso wonders if he has a choice. He can't stay in Cuernavaca anymore. He needs money, a new home, a fresh start.

"And who is he?" Celso ventures again.

After a moment: "My brother."

Celso almost falls off the barstool.

"You have a problem with this?"

"No," says Celso, recovering his composure. "What did he do?"

"*That* you need not know."

"True," muses Celso. "Perhaps it's better that way."

Celso remembers his older brother, Samuel. He was strong and smart. Everyone in Cuernavaca loved him. But Samuel was never very kind to Celso. Teased him. Made him feel ridiculous in front of their friends. Not enough to have him killed, though. If he were still alive, that is.

"But we still have a bargain, correct?" Adolfo prods, trying to hide any concern.

Celso wraps his hands around his beer. "Yes, señor," he says softly. "We have a bargain. You have nothing to worry about."

Still Searching for a Story

Interviewer's notes: **April 8, 2006.** *Lost Souls Café in downtown, off of Fourth Street, turn right down an alley just past Rocket Pizza if you're walking from Spring Street. Hip new coffee and sandwich place, furnished with secondhand furniture, original artwork on the walls, bookshelves filled with literary journals and used books. Excellent lattes. I like this song that's playing; I think it's from the new Beck CD. The guy behind the counter tells me that they pipe in music from KCRW's Web site. Back on track: Moisés Rojo agreed to be interviewed after I explained my rather unpleasant encounter with La Queenie at the Women's Facility. He said he'd be wearing a red, short-sleeve shirt and blue jeans. Ah! Moisés has just entered the café, looks around and sees me. I nod and wave. Not a bad-looking man, considering his age. Looks quite fit. I point to the coffee bar and hold up my cup so he knows that he should get something for himself before we begin. He understands, orders, and comes over. After some initial chitchat, we dive into some real questions.*

Interviewer: Why did you agree to be in this novel?

Moisés: I am retired. Why not?

Interviewer: But you could be doing something else, something fun.

Moisés: Who says this isn't fun?

Interviewer: You do seem content.

Moisés: My ch'i is back in balance, I have corrected the bad feng shui in my life, and I thank the powers that be that my apartment was not built facing a fork in the road, a dead end, or a valley.

Interviewer: You're joking, right?

Moisés: Next question.

Interviewer: Do you love Conchita?

Moisés: Ay, mujer, you don't beat around the bush.

Interviewer: No reason to. Do you want to answer the question?

Moisés: Only if you answer one for me.

Interviewer: Only one.

Moisés: Deal.

Interviewer: Shoot.

Moisés: Have you ever been in love?

Interviewer: [*Coughs*]

Moisés: Well?

Interviewer: Depends.

Moisés: On what?

Interviewer: On how you define *love*. I mean, I've been with men, of course. Dated a lot. Since I was fifteen. I always had a boyfriend. I'm in between men right now. Did I love any of them? That's a hard question.

Moisés: Exactly.

Interviewer: Okay, I get your point.

Moisés: Ah, brilliant as you are beautiful.

Interviewer: No need to flatter.

Moisés: I thought you'd ask me about my, uh, special skill.

Interviewer: What? Oh. Yes, the levitation.

Moisés: Yes.

Interviewer: No. That's nothing more than a metaphor.

Moisés: For what?

Interviewer: Not certain. Olivas never told me. But you know fiction writers. Everything has a double meaning. Symbols, similes, metaphors. Like that paperboy he wrote into this novel. I mean, when was the last time you saw a paperboy? Adults now do that job, driving around L.A. tossing newspapers before the sun rises. Novel writing. Nothing like journalism where we deal with reality.

Moisés: Reality?

Interviewer: Yes, reality.

Moisés: Like what we're doing now?

Interviewer: All right, I promised to move on to something a bit more concrete.

Moisés: ¡Perfecto! I'm ready.

Interviewer: Did you ever expect to meet someone like Conchita? I mean, after your wife died?

Moisés: [*Laughs*] That's more concrete?

Interviewer: I think so.

Moisés: Fine. Well, let me put it this way: Conchita is like no other. Even now, I'm surprised by her.

Interviewer: How?

Moisés: It's difficult to put into words.

Interviewer: Try, please.

Moisés: She makes me think. She questions my beliefs, makes me explain myself. Just when I'm feeling superior, Conchita brings me down to earth, so to speak.

110

Interviewer: But a good friend could do those things.

Moisés: Yes. She is a good friend. My best friend. But there's something else, too.

Interviewer: Yes?

Moisés: Have you ever made love to someone and felt as if you no longer existed?

Interviewer: Ah! So you do love her.

Moisés: Well, have you?

Interviewer: We made a deal. You had only one question for me. No more.

Moisés: Deals may be renegotiated.

Interviewer: This is not about me. It's about you.

Moisés: It sounds like it's about Conchita.

Interviewer: I have an assignment to interview people who appear in this novel.

Moisés: Why?

Interviewer: Kind of a "special features" for the readers.

Moisés: Do they pay you well for this?

Interviewer: Enough. Freelancers have to cobble together a livelihood to keep body and soul together.

Moisés: Ah! You've answered more than one question. So, I guess we've renegotiated our deal.

Interviewer: [Sighs] Though you're more pleasant than La Queenie, you're not much more helpful, I can say that.

Moisés: Lo siento. I didn't mean to give you a hard time. You see, I find it all sort of funny. You and your questions. But I can try to answer.

Interviewer: Please.

Moisés: Sí. Okay, look, I do love Conchita.

Interviewer: I thought so.

Moisés: Was that such a mystery?

Interviewer: But how do you compare this new love with what you had for your late wife?

Moisés: Why would you want to compare?

Interviewer: It's natural, isn't it? I mean, if I'd been married for decades to one person—who eventually dies—and then I fall in love with another, I'd compare the two experiences. How could I not?

Moisés: Do you often entertain such destructive thoughts? I hope not.

Interviewer: There's nothing destructive about it. Maybe it's a gender thing.

Moisés: No, it's a *you* thing. Don't blame such silliness on your gender.

Interviewer: I'm blaming it on your gender, not mine.

Moisés: It's not like comparing the food at different restaurants. One love stands by itself without comparison to another. This is no obfuscation, I assure you. A little knowledge comes with age and experience. Perhaps not much. But enough.

Interviewer: I'm not that young.

Moisés: If you're under thirty—which I suspect is the case—you're young to me. A mere baby.

Interviewer: I know plenty of older people who aren't that wise. Living doesn't necessarily teach you anything. Some people make the same mistakes over and over and over. Right?

Moisés: I don't disagree. I was just trying to make a point.

Interviewer: Take my father, for example. He tried to make it big by selling these silly little gizmos for the kitchen. He maxed out his credit cards, mortgaged our house in Baldwin Park, sank everything into his business. And you know what? He lost everything.

Moisés: I'm so sorry.

Interviewer: And do you know what he did when he finally got us back on track financially?

Moisés: I can guess.

Interviewer: He did it again, that's what. This time it wasn't little toys for the kitchen. No, he invented, well, never mind. I don't want to get into this.

Moisés: Are you okay?

Interviewer: Look, it appears that you don't want to answer my questions. This is going nowhere fast. Maybe we should call it a day. I have others who would be happy to talk with me.

Moisés: My dear, whatever you wish. I don't intend to be rude or uncooperative. I'm just trying to be true to myself. Could you ask for anything but the truth?

Interviewer: Of course I want the truth.

Moisés: You are a lovely and intelligent woman.

Interviewer: Again, please don't bother with the flattery.

Moisés: Put down that pen and let us have a real talk over our delicious coffees.

Interviewer: About what?

Moisés: About love, of course. Love. Does anything else matter?

Interviewer: I can think of several things, actually.

Moisés: Ah! You've answered my question, finally!

Interviewer: Which question?

Moisés: [*Laughs*] Have you ever been in love?

Interviewer: Oh, that question.

Moisés: I now know that you have not.

Interviewer: How?

Moisés: If you've experienced love, even lost it—especially if you've lost it—you could never imagine anything to surpass it.

Interviewer: You're a foolish old man, do you know that?

Moisés: That, too, is true, my dear. That, too, is true.

A Gift for an Angel

It had been three months since Jacob Salcedo last set eyes on Conchita. He'd been delivering newspapers in her neighborhood for almost a year, but usually didn't see his customers because of the time he did his job. But this one morning, Jacob saw Conchita waiting by her door. Waiting for him. The boy hadn't known that Conchita couldn't sleep that night, tossed and turned with dark dreams, and that finally, at 5:30 a.m., she'd given up and wanted to read the newspaper with an earlier-than-usual breakfast. That morning three months ago, Jacob was about to toss the newspaper but stopped, with a little skid of his tires, as Conchita smiled and walked up to him.

And Jacob had smiled back, dumbstruck, at this older woman who, at that moment, looked like an angel in her flowered robe and fluffy, red slippers. She'd introduced herself and thanked the boy. Nothing more. But the rest of Jacob's route was filled with delicious memories of her smile.

Jacob hadn't seen her since. Each morning, he slowed down as he approached Conchita's duplex. Nothing. The boy's memory of that one meeting expanded and became more elaborate with time until finally Jacob remembered hours of imagined conversation with this angel. *His* angel. An imagined conversation that covered many topics from world events—Jacob could opine on every complex political issue, to the amazement of Conchita—to his mother who refused to leave their house because she believed that a man stalked her, and about Jacob's father, who tried his best to keep his little family intact, fed, and safe even though his wife grew more frightened and withdrawn by the day. Jacob's fantasy started to stale, however, and he grew impatient at not seeing Conchita again.

So one cool, clear morning, Jacob decided to offer a little hello. He laid his bicycle gently on the small lawn in front of Conchita's duplex, pulled out a rolled-up newspaper from his large bag, and set the paper standing on end in the middle of the cement walkway. It took a few tries to erect it but he eventually succeeded. Jacob heard a stirring behind the front door, a click of the doorknob. What should he do? Suddenly, Jacob panicked, felt silly, his face burning in shame. He scrambled onto his bicycle, almost falling, and pedaled as fast as he could. Jacob wondered what Conchita would think of his little offering. He felt so stupid! How could anyone imagine that his ridiculous stunt was a gift?

When he was about a house away, Jacob turned. He saw Conchita laughing, bending down to retrieve the newspaper. He turned away and smiled to himself. Jacob had seen the face of an angel again. A face filled with joy because of his gift. A face he would always remember.

A Rose by Any Other Name

Sarkis sighed. "Leonard, look at this."

Leonard walked into their study and looked over Sarkis's shoulder. "What am I looking at?"

"Read what Conchita wrote."

Leonard put his hands on Sarkis's shoulders, leaned toward the computer screen, and squinted. After a few moments, he let out a little laugh.

"She named a whippet after you? What an honor."

"An honor? How would you like to have a dog named after you?"

Leonard thought for a moment.

"Well?"

"I don't think that 'Leonard' would make such a good name for a dog, let alone a whippet," said Leonard. "But 'Sarkis' works for me."

"Go to hell," said Sarkis as he deleted the e-mail.

"I love you, too," said Leonard as he left the study.

Rolando ♥ Josh

FARMBOY: u ok?
ROLANDO88: thinkin bout stuff
FARMBOY: ur mom?
ROLANDO88: yes
FARMBOY: she luvs ur pop, right?
ROLANDO88: yes
FARMBOY: so don't worry
ROLANDO88: i know
FARMBOY: probably an easy explanation 4 what we saw
ROLANDO88: yes
FARMBOY: so don't worry, promise?
ROLANDO88: ok
FARMBOY: good
ROLANDO88: u know what?
FARMBOY: what
ROLANDO88: i luv u

FARMBOY: :-)
ROLANDO88: i mean it
FARMBOY: i know u do

Grand Central Market

As Conchita got off the crowded bus, she wondered what life would have been like if she'd met Moisés fifty years earlier. Imagine: young people in love, enjoying each other as God had intended, at the budding of their sexual powers. Conchita's heart began to beat hard as delicious, manufactured memories took root in her mind. Not that she didn't enjoy what she and Moisés now took pleasure in: the mature lovemaking of two people who had seen much in life, and who had maybe twenty or so more years left on this earth. Theirs was a full existence, one for which she thanked God whenever she thought about all the suffering in this city, the country, around the world. Conchita read the news as intently as the next person and shook her head in great sadness: drive-by shootings, child abuse, obituaries of young men and women killed in the war, the homeless being poked and prodded by the police in downtown, anti-immigrant groups spewing hate, babies left to die in Dumpsters and open fields. And on and on and on and on and on. Indeed, she felt guilty, at times, for her happiness and overall health. How did God choose which of His children would have good fortune? Harder still to grasp: *Why* did He choose those who would suffer? And why did evil people always seem to prevail? Conchita's mother often said: La mugre siempre flota. Filth always floats. But that was nothing more than Mexican folk wisdom, a little dicho, a bite-size answer to a complex question. In short, a catchy way to explain why the world often seems so unfair. And Conchita knew she wasn't the first person to wonder such things. She'd like to imagine the ancients arguing amongst themselves, trying to understand the way fortune worked, creating numerous gods to help explain the randomness of fate: Quetzalcoatl, Tezcatlipoca, Tlaloc, Cinteotl, and so many others. And these gods were riddled with human faults: jealousy, rage, lust, drunkenness. Nothing new. But it was her turn to confront one of the great mysteries of life. Was there a purpose for everything that happened? Conchita's religion told her, yes, there is a reason for it all but we're too simple to understand God's ultimate, magnificent plan. She could try to find comfort in this but it was no use. Conchita found no solace in mystery. When she was young, she always wanted to know how the traveling magicians did their tricks. Conchita could never stomach inscrutability in any form.

Conchita's mind swirled with conflicting thoughts of lovemaking and world-weariness, inspiration and defeat. Did God have a plan? Or could life simply be a series of random events? Was it random that Conchita had taken Sarkis out for a walk and discovered that poor little neighbor girl, Sofia, standing naked in that horrible man's house? What if Conchita had decided to delay taking Sarkis out? Sofia might still be there with that man or worse. Conchita stopped by a row of news racks and examined the headlines. The *Los Angeles Times* had a large photograph of Mayor Villaraigosa, smiling, shaking hands, celebrating his agreement with legislators and teachers to reform the city's schools. ¡Ay! Another problem that preyed on her mind as she tried to sleep at night: the schools! Well, at least someone was trying to do something. Conchita leaned down and squinted at the newspaper through the cloudy plastic. Not a bad-looking man, either, she pronounced in a whisper. Young, too. He could go very far. She stood up and said to herself: Senator Villaraigosa. No, wait: *President* Villaraigosa! Sounds good. Perhaps someday the country would be ready for a Chicano president.

Conchita looked at her watch. Lunchtime. Grand Central Market was but a block away. A full stomach would help her complete the shopping she needed to do. Moisés would have a birthday soon and she wanted to make this gift special though Conchita had no idea what to get. As she made her way, the streets seemed more crowded than usual. Two laughing teenage boys approached her. One of them wore a tight, green T-shirt with the words FRANKLY, MR. SHANKLY printed across his narrow chest. The other boy's white T-shirt had the large, blue initials F.T.P. emblazoned across his chest just above a caricature of President Bush. The boys separated slightly to make room for Conchita but the passage was too small for her. They brushed by her, one boy on each side, and continued the laughing conversation as if Conchita didn't exist. She blinked, looked the boys up and down, and expected an apology. But none came. The boys were lost in the crowd within seconds. An old borracho whistled at Conchita and said something that sounded obscene but the booze slurred the man's words so that she couldn't be certain. An electronics store blasted Celia Cruz at such a high volume that the singer's deep, experienced voice became nothing more than painful vibration. Conchita covered her ears and wondered how anyone could do that to wonderful Celia.

When she finally arrived at Grand Central Market, the crowds were even larger. Normally Conchita wouldn't have cared but today she felt a bit drained and not quite ready to deal with so many bodies. No matter. Time to eat. And maybe a cup of coffee afterwards would help bring her back to life. She made her way to her favorite food stand, Roast to Go. What should she have? Too · many wonderful choices: carnitas, chicken, lamb, fish, sausage, tripe. Her mouth watered. It all looked so wonderful. When her turn came, she simply closed her eyes and let her inner self choose. Lamb! Yes, that would be perfect. She opened her eyes and ordered. The middle-aged man behind the counter smiled at her, winked, appreciated her looks, no doubt. He was new here. Not bad-looking. But a big, fat wedding ring adorned his left hand. Does his wife know that he's flirting with a mature woman who just ordered lamb for lunch? Likely not. But no harm in smiling back. It's food, not sex, after all.

Conchita lucked out: An old woman had just finished a bowl of posole. This kind soul noticed Conchita searching for a table and motioned her over.

"I'm ready to leave," she said. "Take a seat. Or else you'll be searching for a lifetime."

Conchita smiled and obliged. She set her plate and drink down and settled in. The old woman admired Conchita's choice of lunch.

"Oh, I should have ordered the lamb," she said.

"I'm sure your posole was quite good," said Conchita, trying to be pleasant to the old woman.

"Too watery," she said and made a face that reminded Conchita of those odd dolls whose faces are made of carved, dried apple flesh. "Not a good batch." And then she leaned in and whispered: "They're probably trying to save money by adding water."

With that, the old woman stood and smiled at Conchita. "Today is my birthday," she announced, seeming to forget about the disaster with her lunch choice.

"Oh! How wonderful," said Conchita. "Birthdays are to be cherished."

The old woman's smile broadened. Conchita noticed that she had but four or five teeth left in her mouth.

"Sixty-eight today!" she said, flapping her arms up and down as if she planned to take flight.

Conchita almost let out a cry of shock. She and this woman were just a few years apart. How could this be? Conchita still could get whistles from men, albeit older men than before. This woman looked like a frail grandmother.

The woman pointed to Conchita: "*You* are young."

Conchita blinked.

"And I have but one bit of advice for you."

Conchita listened.

The woman said: "Do not go through life believing that it means anything."

"What?"

"Life is meaningless," the woman continued, without malice, speaking clearly, still smiling. "We are put here to slog our way through each day, suffer, maybe enjoy a nice bowl of soup every now and then, and when our time is up, that's it. Nothing. It's gone." The woman tried to snap to emphasize this last pronouncement but failed to make a noise with her thin fingers.

"No," said Conchita. "Let me tell you that you're wrong."

"What do you know?" said the woman with a resignation not unlike an adult admonishing a confused child. "You're but a young woman with many years left. What could you possibly understand about life? You couldn't possibly have experienced what I have."

Conchita smiled. Young? Yes. Young. Why not?

The old woman and Conchita stared at each other in silence. What could this poor soul be thinking to believe that life had no reason? What kind of path has she walked down all these years to bring her to this conclusion? Has she ever known love? Did she ever marry, have children? Is her husband now dead so that she spends her days all alone? These and other tragic thoughts filled Conchita's head.

Finally, the old woman picked up her large, heavy purse, nodded, and walked slowly away toward the Hill Street exit. It appeared to Conchita that the woman suffered great pain with each step: She moved as if walking through many inches of snow. Conchita kept her eyes on her until the woman disappeared from sight. Conchita turned back to her plate. The lamb looked succulent, perfect. She tore a corn tortilla in half and scooped up several morsels of meat along with some rice and beans. As she bit into the tortilla and let the wonderful flavors and textures mingle upon her tongue, Conchita believed that she had, in fact, made a perfect choice for lunch.

Epilogue

A darkened bedroom, sparsely and neatly furnished in Asian-inspired furniture. Conchita straddles Moisés, the bed a jumble of sheets and blankets. They move in the final throe of making love. Conchita is loud, expressive, while Moisés is controlled, almost silent. Conchita finishes with a yelp, drops her face onto Moisés's chest, and listens to his heart for a few moments before sliding off and landing with a little grunt on her side of the mattress.

Conchita, out of breath: I want.
Moisés: You want what, mi amor?

Conchita readjusts herself and makes a pillow of Moisés's flat stomach. She plays with the white and black curly hairs that peek from beneath the sheet. Moisés squirms, muffles a laugh.

Moisés: Tickles!
Conchita: Yes.
Moisés: So, what do you want, mi amor?
Conchita: I just want.
Moisés, laughing: We all just want, ¿no?
Conchita: Yes, but I *want*.
Moisés: Oh, that's different, mi amor. Why didn't you say so before?

Conchita climbs back on top of Moisés, straddling him, and crosses her arms defiantly.

Conchita: What do you want?
Moisés, serious: I want people to stop killing other people.

Conchita falls forward and plants both palms on either side of Moisés's head. He turns to the left and then the right examining his beautiful prison.

Conchita: No, really.
Moisés: Really. Es cierto, mi amor.

Conchita falls onto Moisés's chest, snuggles tightly.

Conchita: That is a good thing to want.
Moisés: It's *one* thing to want.
Conchita: Sí.
Moisés: I also want a 1974 Maserati Khamsin.
Conchita: A what?
Moisés: But only a few hundred Khamsins were produced. So I'm more likely to get people to stop killing each other. And what do you want?
Conchita, laughing softly: I want everything. Everything that makes life beautiful.
Moisés, studying Conchita, nods: *That* is a good thing to want.

Conchita extricates herself from Moisés and stands. She walks to the bathroom and closes the door. After a few moments, the toilet flushes, water runs, and then silence. Moisés looks expectantly at the bathroom door. One moment, then another, pure silence, and still no Conchita. Moisés gets restless. He turns to the clock on the nightstand. The glowing numbers read 2:47 a.m. Moisés sighs and turns back to the bathroom door. Finally, the doorknob turns and Conchita comes back to bed. She resumes her place next to Moisés. Relieved, he pulls her close.

Moisés: Are you okay, mi amor?
Conchita: Por supuesto.
Moisés: Really?
Conchita: Sí.
Moisés: Happy?
Conchita: Sí.
Moisés, kissing Conchita's forehead: Good. That is what I want. I want you to be happy.
Conchita: That, and world peace.
Moisés: I didn't say world peace.

Conchita: Yes you did.

Moisés: No, I said I want people to stop killing other people.

Conchita: That's world peace.

Moisés: Perhaps.

A word about Conchita and Moisés. The audience should not assume that these characters represent anything but themselves. They are not archetypes, paradigms, or metaphors for anything beyond themselves. They want comfort, love, sex, good food, etc. Nothing magic, there. Yes, Moisés professes to want killing to stop. Most people want that, to be sure. Not all, but most. In any event, Conchita and Moisés will continue to live their lives together, never marrying because neither needs to. Conchita will eventually die first, many years from now, making Moisés curse God for taking another woman from him. But this is normal, such anger when we lose someone we love. ¿No?

Moisés: Good night, mi amor.

Conchita, kissing Moisés's chest: Buenas noches.

Moisés: Buenas noches.

They snuggle tightly into each other, Conchita's head resting on Moisés's chest. Moisés lets out a loud sigh. Conchita does the same. A dog starts to bark. Moisés lifts his head, alert, ready to get out of bed. He recognizes the dog: It's Sarkis over at Conchita's place. But it stops barking. Conchita starts to say something, but then stops, remains silent. Moisés puts his head back down on the pillow and closes his eyes. Conchita gently pats her lover's chest, as if calming a restless baby. Stage goes dark.

121

About the Author

Daniel A. Olivas is the author of five books of fiction including *Anywhere But L.A.: Stories* (Bilingual Press, 2009), *Devil Talk: Stories* (Bilingual Press, 2004), and a children's book, *Benjamin and the Word / Benjamín y la palabra* (Arte Público Press/Piñata Books, 2005). His writing has appeared in many publications including the *Los Angeles Times, El Paso Times, MacGuffin, Exquisite Corpse, THEMA, The Jewish Journal,* and *La Bloga*. Olivas's work has been widely anthologized including in *Sudden Fiction Latino: Short-Short Stories from the United States and Latin America* (W. W. Norton, 2010), *Social Issues Firsthand: Hate Crimes* (Greenhaven Press, 2007), and *Love to Mamá: A Tribute to Mothers* (Lee & Low Books, 2001). He is editor of *Latinos in Lotusland: An Anthology of Contemporary Southern California Literature* (Bilingual Press, 2008), which brings together sixty years of Los Angeles fiction by Latino and Latina writers. Olivas received his B.A. in English literature from Stanford University and law degree from the University of California at Los Angeles. Since 1990, he has practiced law with the California Department of Justice in the Public Rights Division. Olivas grew up near downtown Los Angeles and now makes his home with his wife and son in the San Fernando Valley.